ALSO BY BF

THE LOST LEVEL SERIES

The Lost Level • Return to the Lost Level • Hole In the World

THE LEVI STOLTZFUS SERIES

Dark Hollow • Ghost Walk • A Gathering of Crows
Last of the Albatwitches • Invisible Monsters

THE EARTHWORM GODS SERIES

Earthworm Gods • Earthworm Gods II: Deluge
Earthworm Gods: Selected Scenes From the End of the World

THE RISING SERIES

The Rising • City of the Dead
The Rising: Selected Scenes From the End of the World
The Rising: Deliverance

THE LABYRINTH SERIES

The Seven • Submerged

THE CLICKERS SERIES (with J.F. Gonzalez)

Clickers II: The Next Wave • Clickers III: Dagon Rising
Clickers vs. Zombies • Clickers Forever

THE ROGAN SERIES (with Steven Shrewsbury)

King of the Bastards • Throne of the Bastards
Curse of the Bastards

NON-SERIES

Alone • *An Occurrence in Crazy Bear Valley* • *The Cage* • *Castaways*
The Complex • *The Damned Highway* (with Nick Mamatas)
Darkness on the Edge of Town • *Dead Sea* • *Entombed* • *Ghoul*
The Girl on the Glider • *Jack's Magic Beans* • *Kill Whitey*
Liber Nigrum Scientia Secreta (with J.F. Gonzalez) • *Pressure*
School's Out • *Scratch* • *Shades* (with Geoff Cooper)
Silverwood: The Door (with Richard Chizmar, Stephen Kozeniewski, Michelle Garza, and Melissa Lason)
Take The Long Way Home • *Tequila's Sunrise* • *Terminal*
Thor: Metal Gods (with Aaron Stewart-Ahn, Jay Edidin, and Yoon Ha Lee)
Urban Gothic • *White Fire*

COLLECTIONS

Blood on the Page: The Complete Short Fiction, Vol. 1
All Dark, All the Time: The Complete Short Fiction, Vol. 2
Love Letters From A Nihilist: The Complete Short Fiction, Vol. 3
Trigger Warnings
Where We Live and Die

UNSAFE SPACES

BRIAN KEENE

Unsafe Spaces is a collection of essays, satire, and opinion regarding writing, the horror genre, the publishing industry, pop culture, current events, and people in the public eye. Any resemblance to persons real or imagined (with exception to satire) is purely coincidental.

Unsafe Spaces © 2020 by Brian Keene

Cover illustration © 2020 Kealan Patrick Burke

The material in this book was first published at Brian Keene.com between 2014 and 2016, with the following exceptions:

"Once More, With Feeling: Some Thoughts on Jack Ketchum's *The Girl Next Door*" is original to this collection; "Going to Extremes: Some Thoughts on Extreme Horror" is original to this collection; "Eulogy for Jesus's Memorial Service" is original to this collection; "Guns" is original to this collection; "Success Changes" is original to this collection; "Unsafe Spaces" is original to this collection; "A Remembrance of J. F. Gonzalez" first appeared in *Fangoria Magazine*, 2014; "The Scariest Part" first appeared on Nicholas Kaufmann's website, 2015; "A Remembrance of Tom Piccirilli" first appeared in *Locus Magazine*, 2015; "Family Matters: An Appreciation of Mary SanGiovanni" first appeared in the *2015 NECON Program Book;* "Musings of a Middle-Aged White Guy" first appeared in *The Daughters of Inanna*, Thunderstorm Books, 2015.

ISBN: 9798663393348

CONTENTS

Acknowledgments	xi
Summer	1
Writer Hell	3
Drone / Scars / Magic Sunglasses / Beyond The Comfort Zone	5
New Monsters	8
Once More, With Feeling: Some Thoughts On Jack Ketchum's "The Girl Next Door"	10
Heavy Nostalgia	17
Same As It Ever Was	20
The Mirror	21
A Writer's Prayer	22
Millennial Monsters	24
On Bizarro Selling Out (And Some Advice For New Authors)	26
Infinite You: We All Contain Multitudes	29
On Not Being A Dick	32
Squirrely Speed	34
Sir Joyce And The Gill-Man	37
Wicker Man	40
Dancing In The Ruins And Punching The World While The Real Horror Writers Ply Their Trade	42
Products Of The Times	44
Exorcising Ideas	47
Why Writers Should Ignore Reviews	50
The Leaves Fall Faster	52
In Hwa "Cunt" Is Okay, But "Empathy" Is Not	55
Ebola For Christmas	59
More On BTK And HWA	62
A Captain Marvel For Every Generation	65
Fear Of An Old Planet	67

Going To Extremes: Some Thoughts On Extreme Horror	70
A New Age Of Fuckery	77
Solidarity Isn't Just For Unions	81
iOppression	84
The Secret To Crafting Effective Horror	86
On Wasting Votes	88
People Are People	91
On Literary Estates	93
Matters Of Perspective	96
J.F. Gonzalez R.I.P.	99
A Poem Or Lyrics Or Something That I Wrote While Drinking Last Night	105
Post-Mortem On A Muse	106
A Remembrance Of J. F. Gonzalez	108
Eulogy For Jesus's Memorial Service	110
True Wealth	115
Brian Keene's Rules For A Successful Public Reading	117
The Scariest Part	119
No-Slave Leia	123
To All Things, An Ending	125
From There To Here And Then Back Again	128
What Comes With Autumn	133
Important Things, And Things Less Important	136
A Remembrance Of Tom Piccirilli	138
Family Matters: An Appreciation Of Mary Sangiovanni	140
A Trip To Miskatonic University	144
Dear Rose: An Open Letter To A Fan I Met This Weekend	146
Dust To Dust	149
Now Leaving The Complex	156
The Samhain Blackout: What Was Said And Why It's Important	158
Musings Of A Middle-Aged White Guy	171
Brave New World	176
Normal People's Jobs...And Sleep Patterns	179
Memo From The Sick Bed	181

Some Thoughts On Living And Dying	184
The End Of The Bronze Age Of Superhero Cinema?	187
What Neil Gaiman, Brian Keene, And You Need To Do To Be A Writer	190
Some Observations On Crowdfunding And Social Media	193
I Still Want To Believe	195
The Parable Of Fred And Lucas	197
One Star Civilization	199
Guns	202
Success Changes	205
What It Takes To Be A Bestseller	209
Five Minutes Of Fame, Five Minutes Of Friendliness	211
Why And When I Will Begin Boycotting The HWA	213
A Little Warmth Against The Winter	221
Unsafe Spaces	224
About the Author	229

*This one is for Stephen Kozeniewski ...
"This too, shall pass."*

ACKNOWLEDGMENTS

Thanks to Paul Goblirsch, Leigh Haig, and the rest of the team at Thunderstorm Books; Robert Swartwood; Kealan Patrick Burke; Mark Sylva, Tod Clark, Stephen McDornell, and Mike Acquavella; Mary SanGiovanni; and my sons.

Special thanks to Ben Chapman, Graham Joyce, Jason Parkin, Jesus Gonzalez and Tom Piccirilli. Don't wait up for me, wherever you are. I'll be along sooner or later.

SUMMER

I had another late night of working until four in the morning, and slept until just now (8:56). That's the latest I've gotten up all summer. My normal wake up time is usually five o'clock in the morning. That started when I was a kid, back when if you wanted to watch cartoons, you only had three channels to watch them on, and you had to be up at a specific time or they were gone until the following week.

My six-year old can't fathom this. He can't fathom having only three channels and having to watch programs at a certain time. He can't fathom not having those programs available on demand, at any time that is most convenient for him. He also can't fathom compact discs, rotary phones, or 8-bit video games.

He also doesn't believe that when Daddy was his age, Daddy was up by six o'clock in the summer, and out the door by ten, and riding all over the county on a BMX Mongoose nicknamed the Millennium Falcon, or traipsing through the woods like Aragorn until it got dark. He doesn't believe this, because we don't let our children do that these days. Child protective services would take my child away if he rode his bike unsupervised across the county, and probably rightfully so. This is not the late Seventies or early Eighties, and you do not have to be up at six to watch cartoons, and the BMX Mongoose has been replaced by soccer vans and organized play dates and the woods have been cut down to make room for a row of identical suburban houses starting at a price that the average county resident can't possibly afford.

The coffee is done brewing now, and I must get to work on a short story, but man, do I miss *Land of the Lost* and *Thundarr the Barbarian* and *Hong Kong Phooey*, and I may need to rename my V-8 Olds Aurora the Millennium Falcon.

WRITER HELL

A friend of mine died for a little while earlier this year. I'm not going to mention his name because what I'm about to relate is a pretty personal experience, and I think it should be his to keep.

My friend had a heart attack. It took the paramedics a while to arrive. During that time, his heart wasn't beating. Passerby used CPR to keep the compression on his heart going, but my friend had no pulse. He was clinically dead. When the paramedics finally arrived, they shocked him, and on the ninth try, they got a tiny 'Blip', rather than a flat line. That blip is why they took him to the hospital rather than to the morgue.

Yesterday, I asked my friend, who is a writer and a well-known bookseller, if he remembered anything from while he was dead. He told me that he did remember something, but it wasn't what I was probably expecting. He said that he didn't see Heaven or Hell or any of the other afterlives that supposedly exist. He saw no bright light and no deep darkness. No fire or cold or loved ones or monsters. Instead, my friend remembers flying over the deep forests of North Carolina, and the trees and hills were covered in mist, and he was overwhelmed with regrets and remorse for the things he'd done in life.

And that is why I stayed up writing until 3:30 this morning and didn't wake up until a few minutes ago.

DRONE / SCARS / MAGIC SUNGLASSES / BEYOND THE COMFORT ZONE

I had a REM-less and dreamless sleep last night. I'm so tired this morning that I can barely figure out how to make coffee, let alone type my first thoughts of the day. So I sit here, looking out my window at the world, and my brain is awash in the drone of background noise—the static of the subconscious, the thrum of a rave that was shut down inside my head hours before, but the disc jockey left his equipment on automatic.

This happens more and more as I get older.

Sometimes, if I let my fingertips rest on the keyboard, and tune in to that drone, the words come unbidden, fast and furious, a non-paranormal form of automatic writing.

My carpal tunnel and arthritis are having a team-up this morning. Remember that scene in *Jaws*, when Quint and Hooper are exchanging origin stories for their various scars? (Of course you do. It's the best scene in the film). Well, imagine that scene between two writers. Instead of scars, it's carpal tunnel syndrome, bad backs from sitting all day hunched over a keyboard, and arthritis that transforms their hands into claws. Instead of sharks, or first loves, or Japanese artillery, it's novel titles. "This one right here, Mr. Hooper," Quint says, displaying a hand so bent and gnarled that his fingers won't uncurl, "I got this one from writing *The Labyrinth* series."

Today, after I quit stalling and whining about my aches and pains, I start writing a canon, in-continuity *X-Files* story. I can't tell you much about it, other than that if you like the character of Walter Skinner, you'll like this.

So, I'm sitting here, thinking about that, and waiting for the coffee to brew, and it occurs to me that in today's political climate, both *The X-Files* and *They Live* are absolutely ripe for either a remake or a reboot. Hell, in the case of the latter, I'd argue we are living it. Think about the premise of *They Live*. Now think about the world as it is today. Just replace aliens with globalists, technocrats, and corporate governments. We are in dire need of a billion pair of magic sunglasses. Is there an app for that?

There you go, Hollywood. Remake *They Live* and replace the sunglasses with an iPhone app that tells you how many aliens are around you at any one time. Nick Mamatas and I are available to write it.

Yesterday, I wrote a Bizarro science-fiction/fantasy story, which lead some people to ask, "But why write a Bizarro sf/fantasy story? You're a horror writer."

Well, that's why.

I don't think of myself as a horror writer. I've written crime novels, journalism, political/social non-fiction, and even humor, but because the vast majority of my output has been horror, that's what I'm known for. It's my marketing label. It's also where I'm most comfortable.

But as writers, we need to regularly step outside our comfort zone, or else we risk burning out, repetitiveness, or malaise. Stepping outside that zone makes you a better writer —new ways to practice the old trick of making people uncomfortable with the truths and observations only you can tell.

NEW MONSTERS

I'm back from NECON (Northeastern Writer's Conference), which, along with Scares That Care Weekend, CONvergence, and BizarroCon, remains one of my favorite annual conventions. I had a great time. I sold books. I got a new trophy. I participated in the official roast of my dear friend, author Nicholas Kaufmann. I had a song dedicated and played for me during a concert by Kasey Lansdale. But mostly, I just hung out with good friends. All in all, it was an excellent time. But when I got home last night, there was a hug waiting for me from my six-year old, which was even better.

Next weekend, I'm appearing with fellow author Mary SanGiovanni at the Poe Museum in Virginia. I'm looking forward to that, and to the hug that will be waiting when I get home from that, as well.

This week at home will be spent finishing a vampire short story for Christopher Golden's new anthology. Which brings me to the meat of what I'd like to talk about today. I was on a monster panel at NECON over the weekend. During the panel, my peers and fellow panelists proposed that the "next new monster in horror fiction and film" would spring forth from bio-engineering and GMO foods. A new twist on David Cronenberg's 'Body Horror', if you like. And maybe so. Maybe they are right. After all, Chuck Wendig and Craig Davidson are both already doing some neat stuff in that direction with their most recent novels.

But I think we're also going to see new fictional monsters stemming from the overwhelmingly increasing tribalism that the human race seems content to wallow in. I mean, take a look at us. Turn on your television or your computer or your radio and take a really good look. Everything is Left versus Right. Coke versus Pepsi. Ravens versus Giants. Progressives versus Conservatives. FOX versus MSNBC. Muslims versus Jews. Marvel versus DC.

Everybody shouts at each other until everything comes to a screeching halt. Maybe we are the new monsters. Maybe we continue to build walls around our individual fiefdoms and refuse to consider the other side's views. Maybe we let xenophobia and tribalism turn our society into a post-apocalyptic mirror image of the *Mad Max* movies. Maybe new monsters spring forth as a result.

Every day, I'm told I have to choose a side. And every day I refuse. Neither Coke nor Pepsi. Neither Left nor Right. Neither Marvel nor DC. Neither Fox News nor MSNBC. Neither Rush Limbaugh nor Rachel Maddow. Neither the Ravens nor the Giants. Neither Muslim nor Jew. Neither Catholic nor Protestant. Neither Progressive nor Conservative. And certainly neither Facebook or Tumblr.

Clowns to the left of me. Jokers to the right. Here I am. Stuck in the middle...fuck you.

ONCE MORE, WITH FEELING: SOME THOUGHTS ON JACK KETCHUM'S "THE GIRL NEXT DOOR"

If you think of horror fiction in terms of water, we begin by throwing a rock into a small pool, creating ripples such as the *Epic of Gilgamesh*, *Beowulf*, and Lucian Samosata's *True History*.

The ripples then become waves with Matthew Gregory's *The Monk* (1796), Charles Maturin's *Melmoth the Wanderer* (1820), and of course, the works of Mary Shelley, Bram Stoker, Edgar Allan Poe, Arthur Machen, and others. Those waves increase in size in the decades to follow, with work from such authors as H.P. Lovecraft, William Hope Hodgson, M.R. James, Lord Dunsany, Frank Belknap Long, Robert E. Howard, Clark Ashton Smith, Shirley Jackson, Fritz Leiber, Theodore Sturgeon, John Farris, Robert Bloch, Richard Matheson, Ray Bradbury, Rod Serling, Ramsey Campbell, and so many others.

In the Sixties, contemporary locales such as suburbia become horror fiction's default setting, rather than crumbling waterfront towns and sprawling Victorian mansions. At this point, our waves transform into a tidal wave capable of sinking ships and swamping coastal towns.

Then, with the advent of Stephen King, that tidal wave becomes a fucking tsunami.

The impact Stephen King's work had on the mainstream popularity of horror fiction cannot be understated. (And yes, right now, some of you are hollering, "I thought this was supposed to be about Jack Ketchum's *The Girl Next Door*! What the hell, Keene?" Well, trust me. It is. Just be patient.)

Before Stephen King, horror fiction didn't truly exist. Sometimes it was published as mainstream fiction, or occasionally mystery fiction. More often, it could be found safely ensconced with its siblings, science fiction and fantasy. The trio were considered a genre of one—most commonly referred to as speculative or "weird" fiction. When science-fiction became popular, booksellers and publishers created a marketing category to make it stand out on store shelves. When Stephen King became popular, the same was done for horror. A marketing category was created. Horror was stamped on the spines of books, and readers who were in-between the latest Stephen King or Dean Koontz novels could walk into a bookstore and find an entire genre of books that catered to them. The bookseller's mantra became, "If you like Stephen King, you'll like this."

In terms of marketability and mainstream popularity, 1989 was perhaps horror fiction's high water mark. Every mainstream publisher of note was racing to keep up with the consumers' demands for "more books like Stephen King's" which led to an increase in the number of mid-list paperbacks being published. Often, these paperbacks played to the lowest common denominator, plastering their covers with Day-Glo skeletons, demons, or other garish imagery (that often had nothing to do with the novel itself) with the stated goal of attracting the horror fan. (Two years later, the genre would see the birth of the legendary Dell/Abyss publishing line, which had, in part, hoped to offer a counterpoint to that).

But 1989 offered more than just an ease of availability for horror fiction fans. Not only had horror, as a genre category, been created, but there were sub-genres and factions that catered to a readers' individual tastes. Fans who wanted more mainstream chills, typified by works like Stephen King's (and birthed by previous masters such as Richard Matheson and Rod Serling) found it in the works of writers like F. Paul Wilson, James Herbert, or Robert R. McCammon. Those who preferred the quiet, often literary approach of Shirley Jackson or M.R. James had an abundance of such from authors like Peter Straub, Charles Grant, or T.E.D. Klein. For pulp fans of writers like Robert Bloch or Robert E. Howard, there was Richard Laymon and William W. Johnstone. And those who loved the more lurid thrills offered by writers such as Hugh B. Cave or R. R. Ryan found an evolution among the splatterpunks, as typified by Clive Barker, David Schow, the duo of John Skipp and Craig Spector, or the selected early works of Joe R. Lansdale.

That's where I come in.

In 1989, as a young man in my early-twenties, I was a voracious horror fiction reader, and I bought and devoured all of the above. My tastes were broad enough that I never allowed myself to become pigeonholed into liking one distinct sub-genre. Quiet or splatterpunk, literary or pulp, I read—and enjoyed—them all. But there was something missing. I didn't know what that something was. I couldn't articulate it. But I felt it just the same.

In the early Seventies, comic book scribe Steve Gerber made me want to be a writer. Later that decade, Stephen King made me want to be a horror writer. In the mid-Eighties, it was Richard Laymon's first novel, *The Cellar*, that actually prodded me to believe that I, a lower-middle class kid with no hope of ever going to college, could actually become a horror novelist. And in 1989, it was Jack Ketchum's *The Girl Next Door* that actually showed me how, while simultaneously showing me what had been missing all along.

In his seminal speech at the 1998 Bram Stoker Awards,

author, editor, and scholar Douglas E. Winter stated, "Horror is not a genre. It is an emotion."

Never has this been more apt than when it comes to discussing Jack Ketchum's *The Girl Next Door*.

In 1989, a year when readers could choose between the traditional, literary, suggestively quiet horror typified by Grant, Klein, or Straub, and the artfully-gory, hyper-intensive limitless horror of the splatterpunks, Jack Ketchum's *The Girl Next Door* arrived with (perhaps unknowingly) a middle finger firmly extended to both camps. It eschewed genre subcategories while simultaneously straddling them. The prose was lean when it needed to be (think Laymon by way of Charles Bukowski or Ernest Hemingway), and more expansive and literary when the narrative called for it. There were quiet, heartfelt, descriptive moments (especially at the beginning when protagonist David is introducing the reader to the town and the cast and what life is like for them) but these then give way to some of the most soul-rending physical and sexual atrocities ever committed to the printed page.

Because of the latter, some critics labeled *The Girl Next Door* as a new splatterpunk novel, but it wasn't. While it certainly contained enough violence and blood to qualify as such, it differed on an emotional level from the standard splatterpunk fare. Until that point, even the most exceptional splatterpunk novel (and there were many) had been about art. Splatterpunk's stated intention was that of the court jester, utilizing graphic, extremely gory prose to, as Phillip Nutman put it, "reflect the moral chaos of our times." And while splatterpunk certainly succeeded with blood red colors at doing this, the artistic aspect was always prevalent, and thus, the reader's emotional attachment to the work was often subdued. The best splatterpunk novels were like pretty paintings on the walls. You marveled at their beauty, but you couldn't walk inside the painting and feel them. The same went for the other side of the genre. The quiet, traditional horror, while quite lovely to read, too often felt detached, and hard to connect with emotionally.

Emotion—primal emotion—was what had been missing from much of Eighties' horror fiction, and *The Girl Next Door* brought it in spades. The novel went places that horror fiction simply wasn't supposed to go to, but not just through the physical violence depicted therein. No. It evoked an emotional response in readers that horror fiction had long been lacking. If splatterpunk did indeed reflect humanity's moral chaos, then *The Girl Next Door* was a mirror image of its pathos and sheer nihilism.

The Girl Next Door defied every subcategory that existed within the horror genre, and in doing so, set itself apart as something new. Something different. It wasn't a novel painted in black and white, but in murky shades of gray. And red. There were no good guys. No last minute reprieves. No happy endings. *The Girl Next Door* didn't just break down storytelling tropes and genre expectations—it gutted them in a basement bomb shelter and left them bleeding out on the floor. And in the process, it left many readers feeling the same way.

It left them feeling.

The Girl Next Door wasn't Ketchum's first novel. It was preceded by *Off Season, Hide and Seek, Cover,* and *She Wakes.* Nor was it his goriest novel (at that point, *Off Season* held that distinction). But the emotional gamut that Ketchum puts both the characters and the reader through in *The Girl Next Door* made it *feel* like one of the goriest, most extreme works within the genre to that date.

And that feeling still resonates today.

It resonates every time you read something written by myself. Or Christopher Golden. Or Joe Hill. Bryan Smith. Tim Lebbon. Sarah Pinborough. J. F. Gonzalez. Craig Davidson (who also writes as Nick Cutter and Patrick Lestewka). Carlton Mellick. Tim Waggoneer. Mary SanGiovanni. Cody Goodfellow. Laird Barron. Wrath James White. Geoff Cooper. And so on. Indeed, there are quite literally multiple dozens among today's current generation of prominent horror authors who include *The Girl Next Door* as a major influence on their work. (The only other novels that have had as much influence are Stephen King's *IT* and Joe R. Lansdale's *The Drive-In*). And, as evidenced by the only partial list of authors above, they hail from all of the genre's different and divergent subcategories. And they all agree that *The Girl Next Door* defied those categories, and created something new—a blueprint, from which a new generation of authors often operated.

When I first purchased *The Girl Next Door*, I had no idea of the emotionally-harrowing ride I was about to take. I bought it simply because I'd enjoyed *Off Season* in High School, and it was written by the same guy, and there was a skeleton cheerleader on the cover. Yes, that old Warner Books cover is unfortunate, but it served its purpose at the time—letting young people like myself know that here was a book we might like to read.

And read it I did.

The book left me broken, upon finishing. But it also had me breaking down my own then-meagre attempts at writing, and starting over again, once more with feeling. That had been the missing ingredient. Feeling. And I don't think it's hyperbole to say that, were it not for that novel, I might not be doing this for a living today. And some of the writers I mentioned above, ones who were also inspired by it, have said the same thing about its impact on them.

To learn, years later, that the inspirational basis for the novel stemmed from true events (the Sylvia Likens murder), only enforces the theory that it was a mirror image of humanity's pathos and nihilism. Re-reading the novel after discovering its origin only increases the emotional impact. And re-reading it a third time, years later, as a parent... let's just say I was broken all over again.

Years ago, Jack Ketchum sat in a bar and negotiated my very first novel contract for me (for a book called *The Rising*, which Delirium Books and Dorchester Publishing had both made offers on, for hardcover and paperback, respectively). When he'd finished red-penning the Dorchester contract, Ketchum told me to keep it and use it as a template for every novel contract I'd negotiate in the future. I have done just that, and I will always be grateful to him for that kindness, and the friendship we've developed in years since. But I'm even more grateful to him for writing *The Girl Next Door*. I know what it's like to read it, but can you imagine what it was like to actually write it? The emotional toll must have been devastating at times—but worth it, in the end.

Our genre would be very different without it. And so would the emotional impact that our genre, when at its best, has provided since then.

HEAVY NOSTALGIA

My six-year old was up at six this morning and decided he wanted to read comic books. I've subscribed him to books like *Tiny Titans, Teen Titans Go, Captain Action Cat, Superman Family Adventures*, etc., but I also buy him a lot of Seventies Marvel and DC comics from the quarter bins. He loves the advertisements in those latter—a box of toy soldiers for a dollar, whoopee cushions and x-ray specs, life-size wall posters from *Star Wars, Planet of the Apes*, and a host of vintage *Star Wars* action figures and accessories. Basically, all the stuff I had as a kid. All the stuff that I have to keep explaining to him we can't order for him, because the companies that sold them are long gone now, as are the Marvel and DC who published those comic books originally.

Nostalgia can be a bitter pill.

After reading comic books and eating breakfast, we got on with Batman Day, a nationwide celebration of the Caped Crusader's seventy-fifth birthday. We celebrated by watching *Batman: Brave and the Bold*, listening to my old Power Records Batman book & records that I had as a child, playing with his Batman action figures and playsets, and then heading off to Comix Connection, where he saw cosplayers and got a free mask, cape, and comic (along with the latest issue of *Tiny Titans*, and—for me—the latest issue of *Moon Knight* and the trade paperback of *Jericho Season 4*).

On the way home, my son, who recently just spent a week at Disneyworld and Legoland with his mother, said, "Batman Day is the best day ever!"

And so it was.

I somehow missed the news that Tammy Faye Baker died. Every time I think of her, I can't help but remember her depiction in *Bloom County*. ("I think I'll sing!").

I miss *Bloom County*. It was the absolute lifeblood of my teenage years, and is, along with Hunter S. Thompson, single-handedly responsible for my interest in politics and socio-issues.

If kids today had *Bloom County*...and wow, that sounded old. And that is the problem. Kids today couldn't have *Bloom County*, because the strip was very much a product of its time. Remember Michael Jackson and Ozzy Osbourne's appearances in town, or when Steve Dallas filmed a video with Tess Turbo? Replace those with Beyonce or Robin Thicke or Maroon 5 and hear the vast whooshing sound as the funny is sucked out of it. And while the Bush and Obama administrations are ripe for satire, they would have never responded to *Bloom County* with the self-effacing laughter and good will that Reagan, Carter, Weinberger, Dukakis, and other politicians did. Instead, they'd have drones hovering over the dandelion patch.[1]

We were reading *Bloom County* in high school, but maybe we should have been reading *1984*, instead.

---

1. A year after I wrote this, Bloom County did indeed return, and it is as irreverent and funny and incendiary and heartwarming as ever.

SAME AS IT EVER WAS

Yesterday, Mary SanGiovanni and I were guest speakers at the Poe Museum in Richmond, Virginia. After our talk and signing, we were lucky enough to look through an archive of rare Edgar Allan Poe's manuscripts, notes, letters, and books. Among them was a copy of Poe's first collection, for which he was paid only in copies—twenty-five copies, to be exact. We also saw three issues of *Southern Literary Messenger*, a magazine in which serialized installments of *The Narrative of Arthur Gordon Pym* appeared, for which Poe was paid only $3 per page.

Now, payment in copies and payment per page are nothing new. Many authors still get paid that way today. But when you adjust for inflation, and compare what he got paid back then versus what we get paid now?

Poe was getting paid more.

Good morning, fellow writers. Have a good day at work...

THE MIRROR

Here's something that happens.

You wake up, and you look in the mirror, still half-asleep, and it occurs to you that you're in your mid-forties, and those first forty years? They went by fast. It didn't seem like it, at the time, but when you stop and think about the time span, it went by in a fucking flash, and, given that most folks die in the Seventies or Eighties, your life is more than halfway over.

How fast is the second half going to go?

And yes, you got to see the world and everything in it from Cuba to the Gaza Strip, and touched Stonehenge, and swam in both the Arctic Circle and Loch Ness, and had some great loves, and some worthy adversaries, and did right by your children whom know that you love them, but you never got the chance to buy that van and trick it out like *The A-Team* and travel across the country helping people and having more adventures.

Maybe you should do that today.

Or you could finish this long overdue novel and turn it in.

Your choice.

Tick-tock...

A WRITER'S PRAYER
(NOT TO BE CONFUSED WITH "A WRITER'S PRAYER" BY NEIL GAIMAN)

I started writing seriously (meaning writing with the intent of publication rather than just fucking around) in 1990. I sold my first short story in 1997. I sold my first book in 2001. I've been on the road ever since.

Every year, I spend a portion of my time on tour, signing books, speaking in public, etc. I've signed in forty-five of America's fifty states (plus Washington D.C.) and several locations across Canada, as well. The least amount of signings I ever did in a year was eight. The most I ever did was forty-two.

My favorite tour was the year my former assistant, Big Joe, and I hopped in a car and drove around the country, going everywhere from Georgia to Illinois to California—and everywhere in between. Other favorite tours included the ill-fated one J.F. Gonzalez and I did for *Clickers II*, where every signing but one was met with various disasters and comedies of errors, and the California tour that Mike Oliveri, Michael T. Huyck, Geoff Cooper, Gak, Gene O'Neill and myself did for *4X4*, because it was our first, and it was special.

Much of my career—and indeed, much of my adult life—

has been spent on the road. Those years spent on the road have taken their toll on me, and as I get older, that toll is increasing.

I'm not a religious man, but I am spiritual (as I think most creative people probably are). And while I don't prescribe to any one particular dogma or faith, there is a little prayer (or chant, if you prefer) that I came up with years ago. I always utter it before making a public appearance. It goes, *"May the journey be short, and the line be long."*

After I finish this cup of coffee, I'm flying to Atlanta, Georgia, to be Brian Keene and sign books for people at the Monsterama Convention this weekend.

I hope the journey there is short. I hope the line of folks waiting to get in is long.

According to the news, I'm not the only person flying into Atlanta today. So are two Americans who are dying of Ebola. This is happening because somebody somewhere thinks it's a good idea.

"Let's go pick up two people dying from a highly communicable disease that liquefies your insides and makes you bleed out and for which there is no cure, and bring them back here."

What could possibly go wrong?

I've read that book, and seen that movie, before.

May the journey be short, and the line be long.

MILLENNIAL MONSTERS

I'm home from a convention that focused on "classic" monsters, such as the Universal and Hammer Films' rogue's gallery. Twelve years ago, the horror convention circuit was full of similarly-themed conventions, but you don't see too many of them these days. Bela Lugosi, Vincent Price, Boris Karloff, and the Mummy, the Creature, and Frankenstein have now been replaced by Bruce Campbell, Ken Foree, Kane Hodder, and Freddy, Jason, and Leatherface.

Except that Freddy, Jason, and Leatherface are also now a little long in the tooth. (You'll notice I didn't say that Bruce, Ken, and Kane are longer in the tooth, as well. That's because Ken is a dear friend, and Bruce and Kane are friendly acquaintances, and all three of them could beat me into a bloody pulp without even flexing, and thus I would like to stay on their good side).

If you look at it in terms of classic rock—classic rock used to be the Beatles, the Rolling Stones, and Marvin Gaye. Now, classic rock is Bon Jovi, Prince, and Guns n' Roses. The same can be said of our monsters. Dracula, the Wolfman, and The

Creature from the Black Lagoon used to be classic rock. Now, it's Evil Dead, Friday the 13th, and Texas Chainsaw Massacre.

So who or what are the new monsters? I don't mean the new monsters professionals in our field are dreaming up (which we talked about here a few weeks ago). I'm talking about stars. Who are the new stars? What are the horror movies that have such a shared cultural impact that they can be the foundation of a convention? And what actors and actresses can do the same?

I'm talking about horror films and horror stars who are a draw across a wide range of socio-economic boundaries. What is the new Mummy or Alien? Who are the new Veronica Carlson or Barbara Crampton, or Vincent Price or Sid Haig?

A decade from now, when the millennials are our age, will their classic rock only be zombies and Norman Reedus? We owe them more than that.

This is my fault, isn't it? The fucking zombie thing...?

Last night, the Bizarro Across America tour did a local set here in Central, Pennsylvania. Afterward, most of the authors spent the night at my place instead of getting hotel rooms. And thus, instead of typing loudly this morning and risking waking them up, I'm simply surfing the Internet, and that's how I came across this little gem: Blackie Lawless, the front-man for 80s metal giants W.A.S.P., was originally cast as the T-1000 in *Terminator 2*, but was then replaced by Robert Patrick.

Think about that.

Blackie fucking Lawless could have been a horror icon, signing autographs next to Bruce Campbell and Ken Foree.

ON BIZARRO SELLING OUT (AND SOME ADVICE FOR NEW AUTHORS)

So, last night there was a major kerfuffle online within the Bizarro fiction genre community. Many things were said by many people, and I'm not going to address all of them. Instead, I'm going to address just two:

1. Apparently, some people think the Bizarro fiction genre has "sold out" because established, popular, non-Bizarro authors like myself profess to enjoy it. If you are one of the folks who feel that way, go fuck yourself. Twice. The fact is, I was reading and enjoying Bizarro fiction before it was even called that. I was reading and enjoying it while you were still working your way through *Hop on Pop* and *Green Eggs and Ham*.

I do not claim to be a Bizarro writer. I do not want to be a Bizarro writer. I simply enjoy the genre. I like reading it. I like discussing it. It brings me a vast amount of enjoyment, and thrills and delights me in a way most other fiction doesn't. When I am enthusiastic about something, I tell others about it, because I want to share my enthusiasm with them.

Some of you are upset that author Kelli Owen and I appeared for one night and one show on the Bizarro Across America Tour. You think this is proof that the genre has somehow "sold out". Well, let me educate you on some things. We appeared that night because:

a) I worked in conjunction with the bookstore (The York Emporium) to have the Bizarros there.

b) The whole fucking point of the tour was to introduce Bizarro fiction to people who might not be familiar with it. Kelli and I were on hand to lure hesitant locals who might not otherwise have attended. And guess what? It worked. Hesitant locals showed up because Kelli and I were there. And they listened to the Bizarro authors give readings and do Q&A panels. And as a result, Bizarro fiction picked up a bunch of new readers.

I enjoy reading Bizarro fiction because it offers me an escape. And I enjoy attending BizarroCon because it is the absolute last convention on Earth where I can relax and feel safe and not have to be on and be "Brian fucking Keene" all weekend long. I will continue to support the Bizarro genre, and its authors, and its publishers. I will drag my balls across six miles of broken glass to defend it. If these things upset you, well again, go fuck yourself. If you are so insecure that you react like this the moment a supposedly perceived "straight" reader praises your work, how will you react to other readers when they discover your work as well? Don't you want readers? Which brings me to...

2. During last night's online argument, Kelli Owen was called a 'bitch" for having the audacity to not like a story written by a particular Bizarro author. This is unacceptable for several reasons, but rather than pointing out the obvious sexist and bullying portions of that attack, let me go right to the heart of what inspired it—which was insecurity.

If you want to be a writer—regardless of whether you're writing Dan Brown-level thrillers or Bizarro novellas that will be read by a small cult audience—you need to accept that not everybody is going to like everything you do. Writers write, and unless you are sticking the manuscripts in a locked box upon completion, the public gets to see what you've written once you've finished it. And then they get to comment on it. Sometimes, they will sing your praises and shower your work with accolades, and that feels really good. Other times, they will give it a one-star review on Amazon and say disparaging things about you, and that feels terrible. Either way, they have a right to do this.

Paintings, comics, music, books—these things are art, but if you sell them then they are also commercial products. And when the public spends money on that product, they have the right to comment on it, good or bad.

The Internet age has a saying: "Don't read the comments." I have a saying for authors of the Internet age: "Don't read the reviews."

Don't read the reviews, regardless of whether they are good or bad. If you can't handle them, or worse, if you start believing them, then don't read them. You'll find that this job is a lot easier that way, and your insecurities (which ALL OF US HAVE by the way) will be less likely to rise to the surface and turn you into a raging, bullying, diseased ass-clown who hurts and damages a lot of people who really didn't deserve it while you're flailing around, denouncing sell-outs and commercialism and how nobody understands you.

And one more time, go fuck yourself.

INFINITE YOU: WE ALL CONTAIN MULTITUDES

It feels good to be off the road and done with public appearances for the year. But now there are all sorts of other things to attend to—things that fell by the wayside while I was off signing books. For example, this morning there was no coffee in the house. Which is a crisis of epic proportions.

So, I stumbled to the car and drove to a convenience store to buy some coffee. While I was waiting in line at the store, behind a herd of lemmings all of whom were buying lottery tickets, I saw a guy with a haunted stare. His face spoke of miles traveled. His aura told the toll of those miles. He had prison tattoos on his neck and hands, and he wore a black hoodie that said "PURSUE RIGHTEOUSNESS" and a red ball-cap that proclaimed "JESUS IS MY NEW BOSS AMEN". He bought Gatorade and a pack of cigarettes, which he stuffed into a black, tattered backpack. Then he left the store and walked down the street, probably on his way to work—I'm guessing as a roofer or maybe as a flagger for a road construction crew (given the state of his work boots and the Gatorade purchase). He seemed sad, but determined.

Human beings contain multitudes of characters. Multitudes

of stories. A good writer knows how to spot these different facets and use them later.

Although it shouldn't be news to anyone who has read more than four of my books, a science article making the rounds this morning says that gravity might be the key to proving the incontrovertible existence of parallel worlds and alternate realities.

This is, of course, one of the two central conceits of my fictional Labyrinth mythos. And science is edging closer to proving it. String *Theory* becomes String *Fact*. And this means that somewhere out there in the universe, you got it right. No matter how badly you fucked everything up, there's another you who didn't.

Life doesn't often offer us second chances. But science may soon give us an infinite amount of them.

After I got back from the store, and made some coffee, and woke up a little bit, I took my six-year old fishing. He used a Spider-Man fishing rod that was a gift from a family friend. I used a reliable old fishing rod I've had since I was his age. The tackle box we carried with us has been in my family for three generations. Inside of it were lures and flies that belonged to—and were tied by—my grandfather, my great-uncle, and my father.

While we stood along the bank, my son used a spinner lure that has been in our family since before World War Two. When he got it snagged on a rock, and his line broke, he was quite upset that he'd lost the lure. This gave us an excellent opportunity to take a break and go swimming, and when we did, I rescued the lure from beneath the rock.

My grandfather and my great-uncle are no longer with us, and my dad's days of fishing are over. And yet, in a way, all of us —my grandfather, my great-uncle, my father, my son, and myself—got to go fishing together yesterday.

We all contain infinite multitudes, and we don't have to travel to an alternate universe to be aware of it.

ON NOT BEING A DICK

A few months ago, I wrote an essay decrying misogyny in the fields of horror, fantasy, and science fiction prose, and comic books. That essay has since been republished in *Trigger Warnings*. Since then, I've been called a progressive, a leftist, a feminist, and a huckster simply using the debate for promotional purposes. I'm none of these things. While I certainly lean more toward the Left than the Right on social issues, I'm avowedly and militantly apolitical, and often disagree with the Left and Progressives. And while I have friends among and am often sympathetic with modern day feminism, I think terms like "mansplaining" are sexist and dismissive, and not conducive to establishing a mutual dialogue where women's legitimate complaints (of which there are many) will actually be heard. As for the huckster bit, I've got a dedicated fan base over 100,000 strong. I don't need to promote anything anymore, unless I choose to do so.

You don't need to be a progressive, or a feminist, or a white knight to decry misogyny. All you need to be is human. Threatening violent acts such as rape against someone is wrong. Sexual harassment is wrong. Reacting negatively to someone because of their gender is wrong. If you do these things, you are being a dick.

Another thing I've been hearing is variations of "Okay, we've heard about it already. Why are people still discussing it? Move on. Not all guys in the genre are behaving like dicks." Well, you're right. Folks like myself, Nick Mamatas, Chuck Wendig, John Scalzi, and Greg Rucka have talked about it quite a bit in the last few months—BUT IT'S STILL OCCURRING. Most recently, in the videogame industry. And that's why we will continue to talk about it. As public figures, we have a responsibility to do so. As men who have mothers, or wives, or girlfriends, or daughters, we have a responsibility to do so.

And so do you, because you also have a mother or wife or girlfriend or daughter, and you'd be incensed if some repugnant jackass with the brain of a howler monkey jacking off into a razor-laced grapefruit was following them around online threatening to rape them because they commented on a comic book cover or a video game. And yes, that's a real thing that really happened.

Stopping these cretins is a two-fold process. Part of it involves stronger, better laws governing these things. But the bigger part is making it socially unacceptable, the same way threatening to rape and murder someone over the color of their skin or sexual orientation is unacceptable. And the only way to do that is to be louder than the dickheads.

Want me to shut up about it? Then speak up about it.

SQUIRRELY SPEED

Last night, while you were sleeping, thousands of us watched a militarized police force in Ferguson, Missouri fire sound cannons, flash-bang grenades, tear gas, and rubber bullets into a crowd of peaceful protesters, and into the sides of civilian homes and yards. We watched them arrest legitimate journalists, demand reporters stop filming, etc. We watched all of this via social media, primarily Twitter.

This morning, the mainstream news reported on Ferguson for a few minutes. Most of what we all saw happen last night was not mentioned. Then they went back to reporting celebrity "news".

But we know. Because we saw it happen.

The revolution will not be televised. It will be Tweeted.

And it will happen fast.

Anyway, enough about that. Back to work. Back to writing. In an hour, the sun will be up and I'll go pick up my son.

Right now, I'm watching a squirrel outside my window.

Civilization's collapse seems to have accelerated. Ferguson. Ebola. Gaza. Israel. Russia. Ukraine. Isis. Boko Harum. The coming financial recession that's gonna make our last one seem absolutely benign by comparison. I'd like to be Iron Man and stop these things. But I'm not Iron Man. I'm just a writer.

The squirrel outside can't do anything about disease, war, or social unrest, either. He just goes on doing what squirrels do.

Civilization ain't the only thing taking some hard knocks. I've got family, friends, and loved ones going through various hard times right now, as well—personal apocalypses that, for them, are every bit as powerful as the ones facing our world. I'd like to be Batman and fix everything for them and take their hurts away. But I'm not Batman. I'm just a writer.

The squirrel can't do anything about personal strife, either. He just goes on doing what squirrels do.

And I do what writers do.

And everything seems to be going faster, except my typing speed.

My six-year old starts first grade this morning. I'm not sure how that happened so fast.

I'm going to quit typing about squirrels and leave here in a few minutes. His mom and I will take him in to school today. Then I need to get back to work on this *X-Files* story (which needs some changes made to it at Chris Carter's request) and also on *Libra Nigrum Scientia Secreta* (which I'm writing with J.F. Gonzalez, who's been a little under the weather lately so I'm pulling double duty on it). If there's time, I also need to collate research pics I took in New Jersey's Pine Barrens last weekend, get my suit dry-cleaned for a funeral (for an old non-writer friend of mine whom none of you know—taken from us suddenly last week), reach out to a few world class free-divers (more research for a new novel called *Pressure*), and write a few chapters of a new novel called *Hole in The World*.

But first, I'm going to clutch my coffee and stare out the window at the trees and sky and the squirrel, because my six-year old starts first grade this morning and I'm not sure how that happened so fast.

It feels like everything is speeding up except me.

SIR JOYCE AND THE GILL-MAN

Author Graham Joyce passed away yesterday, after battling lymphoma. He was, of course, a phenomenal writer, but he was also a phenomenal guy. This business—this writing and publishing thing—if you haven't noticed, not everybody gets along with everyone else. But I've never once heard anyone say anything bad about Graham Joyce. He was kind, sweet, and very welcoming to all.

The year my very first book, *No Rest for the Wicked*, came out, I did my very first signing at the legendary Dark Delicacies bookstore in Burbank, CA—an indie shop that caters exclusively to horror fiction and movies. Now, at that time, I was a nobody. Hell, I was less than a nobody. My credits involved a handful of fanzine appearances, for which I'd been paid in copies, and a few bits of writing on prehistoric websites. But the proprietors of Dark Delicacies were nice enough to let me do signing there anyway.

Also signing that day was Graham Joyce. He had a fairly long line of people waiting for him—perhaps two dozen. Maybe more. Meanwhile, as you might expect, I had exactly zero people in my line. But as each person passed through to get their stuff signed by Graham, he made a point of mentioning my book to them, and showing it off, and gently selling a few copies for me. He didn't have to do that. There are many authors who *wouldn't* have done that. But he did, because that's the kind of person he was. He also took the time to answer all my stupid, nervous questions and give me advice.

Graham Joyce lived in the UK, where they still knight people. I don't know what the process is for that, but if anyone from our field deserved to be knighted, I always thought he would have made a fine choice.

So, I was thinking about Graham this morning, but for some unknown reason, I was thinking about Ben Chapman, as well. Ben Chapman played the Gill-Man in *Creature From the Black Lagoon* (and should not be confused with the racist baseball player of the same name). I knew Ben from the convention circuit, and we'd appeared at many of the same events over the years, and shared many conversations in bars and restaurants and taxi cabs and airport shuttles.

Ben passed away back in 2008. I remember a few years before that, he broke his hip during a convention appearance and was hospitalized in Baltimore. While he was convalescing, I got a phone call from him. "The hospital is going to show *Creature*," he said. "You should come." So I did. Baltimore was only a forty-five-minute drive for me, and it's not often that the Gill-Man himself commands your presence.

I got to the hospital. In attendance were me, a horror webhost designer, several nurses, and some kids from the children's ward. Someone had brought a DVD of *Creature From the Black Lagoon*, and they showed it on a small television. From his hospital bed, which they had wheeled out into this room, Ben offered his own DVD commentary track throughout the movie. The kids from the children's ward loved it, as pretty much all kids do upon watching that movie for the first time, regardless of how old you are.

And that's what I'm thinking about this morning.

WICKER MAN

Yesterday, a senior minister in India's government downplayed a horrendous attack in which a young woman was gang-raped to death on a city bus as, quote, "a small incident".

Four days ago, a police officer in Ferguson, Missouri derisively told an African-American woman named Lillian Guthrie to, quote, "Get a job." Lillian is a successful financial analyst.

Last week, soldiers of the Islamic State—ISIS—massacred the Iraqi village of Kocho. After slaughtering every adult male, they transported the women and children to the city of Tal Afar. There, the male children will be pressed into becoming fighters for the group. The women and female children will be forced into sexual slavery or sold on the black market for the same.

For the past several months, the Boko Haram group has been doing the same thing all across Nigeria, abducting young women and little girls, with the intent of a similar fate.

You know what genre fans are talking about this morning? None of the things I listed above. Instead, they've focused their outrage on a variant cover for a Spider-Woman comic book. Because, priorities. And when I suggested this was ludicrous, a horde of Tumblrs and Twitters turned on me, proclaiming me to be the bad guy. This is nothing new.

Sometimes, people can't cope or heal until they have a bad guy who they can point at and say, "It's all your fault." Sometimes, they need somebody to burn inside the wicker effigy, just like the druids of old. Sometimes, it might even be you that they do it to. And that's okay, as long as *you* know you're not the bad guy—and as long as you are fireproof.

I'm Brian Keene. After twenty years in this business, I am made of asbestos.

DANCING IN THE RUINS AND PUNCHING THE WORLD WHILE THE REAL HORROR WRITERS PLY THEIR TRADE

The movie *Beverly Hills Cop* came out the year I graduated High School. It was notable for two things—Eddie Murphy's rising star performance, and its soundtrack. The latter featured, among other gems, a catchy little pop ditty called "Neutron Dance" by the Pointer Sisters.

I've seen the film and heard that song dozens of times since then, but upon watching it last night, two decades and some years later, it occurred to me that happy, bouncy, funky "Neutron Dance" is actually nihilistic and bleak as all fuck. It's a mournful wail against corporate capitalism and the pathos of modern life, with a narrator that's hoping the bombs will fall tomorrow and end this miserable existence. Not bad for Eighties pop music. Not bad for pop music in general.

If that song was recorded today, "Neutron Dance" would just be about who has the biggest butt, or the most money, or the flashiest car, and would guest-star a bunch of rappers you've never heard of, half of whose names begin with 'Lil', and would be sung via auto-tune.

I also watched *The Raid 2* last night. It is one of those rare sequels that is even better than the original (and in this case, the original—*The Raid: Redemption*—was phenomenal). Perfectly choreographed violence, bloody when it needed to be, but not afraid to pull the camera away, either. Great writing. And an incredibly touching scene involving a seemingly homeless assassin paying child support that is, quite simply, the best cinematic moment I've seen this year. After watching it, I believed that I too could singlehandedly beat up an army.

Another 9/11 anniversary is right around the corner, and as they do every year at this time, our national intelligence agencies are warning us that another attack could be "imminent". This year, the attack supposedly involves members of ISIS crossing the Mexican border. As always, no proof is offered, because proof is not the desired effect.

Fear is.

At the same time, the mainstream media and war-hawks in both the Dempublican and Repocrat parties are bellowing for a full-scale war with Russia in the Ukraine, stating that Russia has invaded the Ukraine, and offering the same kind of "proof" as they did for those WMDs that supposedly existed in Iraq prior to the war there. Once again, the desired result is fear.

This is the time of year when horror novelists such as myself take a break, and focus on other things, while the real horror authors—the ones in Washington and behind the desks at the corporations and the financial institutions—go to work. The kind of fear I offer is one of entertainment. It gets you through study hall or your commute. The kind of fear they offer convinces you to willingly change your lifestyle and give up a little bit more of your rights each time.

In the end, which one is more effective?

PRODUCTS OF THE TIMES

Throw a rock on Tumblr (or better yet, simply surf the web at random) and you're bound to find a Blogger who is outraged over something in pop culture. This morning, I've seen outrage over the inherent racism in everything from the works of H.P. Lovecraft to movies like *The Breakfast Club* and *Ferris Bueller's Day Off*. I've seen outrage over the Seventies sexist depictions of Ms. Marvel and She-Hulk. And I've seen some sort of vague, ill-explained outrage over old Hanna-Barbara cartoons that I gave up on trying to understand.

And all of that is just this morning.

I agree with some of these things (Lovecraft was certainly a racist, and that's just the tip of the iceberg when it comes to the old gent). Other things I don't agree with so much (yes, perhaps *The Breakfast Club* is guilty of whitewashing, but as someone who was in high school when *The Breakfast Club* came out, I can tell you it wasn't far-fetched to have a high school with no black students, as I came from one myself).

Racism, sexism, and other bad things exist. And yes, they often exist in pop culture. There's no denying that. They are indefensible. Inexcusable. But it's also important to remember that in many cases, they are products of their times—times in which institutionalized racism and sexism were entrenched in the culture and in society. That's not an excuse. But it is a fact.

I graduated high school in 1985 at the age of seventeen. I had four friends in my graduating class who were gay. All of them were closeted, except to a small handful of us whom they trusted. They were products of their times. There were no gay pride parades in Central Pennsylvania. There were no shows like HBO's wonderful *Looking* or the less-than-wonderful *Will & Grace*. There was no Anderson Cooper or Rachel Maddow or Neil Patrick Harris (well, we had Neil Patrick Harris, but he was still closeted in those days). Pop culture back then was a product of its time, and if my gay friends wanted to look to a public figure to identify with, they pretty much only had the safe whitewashed androgyny of Boy George, George Michael, or (if you wanted to live dangerously) Elton John, who had come out as bi. It was a very different environment back then—a product of its times, just as things like HBO's *Looking* or the success of Anderson Cooper or Ellen DeGeneres are products of our time.

Today's outrage culture is also a product of its time. And in my lone opinion, it needs to stop focusing its outrage on the past, and focus instead on the now. Yes, H.P. Lovecraft was a racist, and yes, there are no black people in *The Breakfast Club*, and yes, She-Hulk was created to preserve a trademark for Marvel Comics rather than as a bastion of Seventies feminism. These things are all true. But these things are also all in the past. You can't go back and change them now.

Instead of focusing your outrage and derision and snark on things of the past, would it not be better to focus them on the now? Instead of creators taking to Tumblr and Twitter and spending hours deriding a product of institutional racism or sexism that is well past its expiration date, would it not be more productive for creators to spend those hours creating new things—pop culture icons born out of this outrage? Pop culture icons that reflect the now? Pop culture icons that are a product of our times?

Many years ago, when my novel *Dead Sea* first came out, all interviewers wanted to ask me about was why I'd made the main character a gay black man. What was I trying to say with that? And they seemed perplexed by my answer that I wasn't trying to "say" anything—I was simply trying to reflect my audience, not all of whom are straight white men, and I thought it would be nice if I gave them a character whom they could identify with. Years later, when I wrote *Alone*, those same interviewers never once asked about the fact that the protagonists are a married gay couple with an adopted daughter. Why? Because the times are changing, and the products reflect it.

Yes, if you look to the past, you'll see racism and sexism and other inequalities everywhere—products of their times. I'm not suggesting we ignore the past or stop talking about it. But I am saying that you can't change the past, and it seems futile to rail against it, when instead, that energy could be used to reflect the now, so that in fifty or a hundred years, fans have something better to say about the products of our time.

EXORCISING IDEAS

Earlier this week, a reader asked me via Twitter, "What steps do you use to get an idea from your head and on to paper?"

The first thing you need to know is that every author is going to answer this question differently. There really is no "wrong" way to do this—unless your method isn't working for you, in which case it probably is the wrong way and you should try a different method.

What follows is my method, and it's one that has worked for me for many years.

I never start with just the idea. I always need the idea, the first sentence, and a feel for who my main character is before I start writing. Because of this, the idea itself will float around in my head for weeks, months, and—in a few cases—years before I start working on it.

Here is an example. Back in the late-Nineties, I was driving up the East Coast to see my oldest son (who was then just a little guy). A terrible snowstorm hit, and they shut down the highway. A state trooper told me to get off the road, and I assured him I would. After he was out of sight, I continued on my way. I thought to myself, "A blizzard and the cops won't stop me from seeing my son. What would? A nuclear war? No. A zombie apocalypse? No, but that would make a kick-ass novel."

And then...BOOM. Like a bolt of lightning, there was the idea. A father trying to reach his son during the zombie apocalypse. Next came the character. In this case, that was easy. The character was a version of me. Oh, maybe not one-hundred percent me, like Adam Senft from *Dark Hollow* or Timmy Graco from *Ghoul*, but enough of me that I could imbue him with my own thoughts and hopes and fears.

The opening sentence came a few weeks later. And once I wrote that first sentence, it eventually turned into a novel called *The Rising*.

Here's another example. Earlier this year, while on a publicity tour, I got stuck in Oregon for an extra day, and decided to walk around the little town I was in and explore it a bit. In doing so, I decided that I'd love to set a story in that town, so I jotted down a bunch of notes—just rough impressions of geography, local establishments, the demeanor of the people there, and other things I found interesting or that might later inform the setting. And even though I didn't have a story idea or know what the story was about, I had an opening sentence (inspired by some trees that I saw).

That is a big problem for a writer. I had no idea and no character to go with it. All I had was the setting and a possible first line.

A few months later, my old friend Christopher Golden asked me to write a vampire story for an anthology he was editing. I came up with an idea, and then, after considering it further, I realized that it fit perfectly into that setting. Even better, the opening sentence I'd come up with also worked in the context of the tale. That story became "The Last Supper".

I'm a big proponent of the school of thought which states that good ideas will stay with you no matter how long it takes to write them down, and that bad ones will dissipate. In the twenty years I've been doing this, I've been lucky enough to turn forty plus ideas into books or novellas, another hundred plus into short stories, and another thirty or so into comic books. That's approximately one-hundred and seventy ideas that made it to paper. I guarantee you there are twice that many ideas that never did, and never will, because I've forgotten them. I don't write them down because I believe that in doing so, you lose some of your investment in them. Ideas need time to grow—at least for my muse—and growing is an organic process. Writing them down lessens that process for me. It's the difference between a farmer like my father was (in his spare time), and the big GMO factory farms we have today. There are also ideas floating around in my head simply because I haven't had time to write them yet. The good ones will stay there, until I find the time to do so. The bad ones will eventually dissipate back into the Idea Space, where another artist may tap into them and do something better with it than I could have.

So, experiment and find out what method works for you. But in the end, getting that initial idea out on paper really is just as simple as getting it out on paper. Write it down. Write it out. Then keep writing, until you have a story or a novel.

Then get another idea and start on it.

WHY WRITERS SHOULD IGNORE REVIEWS

Yesterday, I told a friend that after forty-five books, three dozen comic books, and two film adaptations of my work, I ignore all reviews, both good and bad. Doesn't matter if they are five-star or one-star—I ignore them all. I wrote about this earlier in the year, but I guess I need to expand upon it.

Reviews are written for consumers. They are supposed to help consumers make an informed decision about their purchase. Creators should ignore them for several reasons.

First, a writer should always be writing for themselves, and never for audience edicts or demands, because that way lies madness.

Secondly, there is a constant danger of believing the reviews, be they good or bad. In the case of the former, the writer may soon believe themselves to be at the top of their game, having mastered their craft, with no further room for growth. This is stupid, because you NEVER master this craft completely, and there is always room for growth. In the case of the latter, a good writer might believe the one-star brigade, and it might impact them to the point where they second-guess everything they do, or worse, quit writing altogether.

The only time I use reviews is when I'm marketing or promoting something. If I'm trying to convince consumers to purchase my new book, then of course I'll point to a particularly enthusiastic review. But when it comes to writing and the creative process itself? I listen to editors and pre-readers and, most importantly, myself.

THE LEAVES FALL FASTER

I spent the last three days enjoying some downtime in Ocean City, Maryland with my girlfriend, where there was no Wi-Fi (which is why you had no updates here). Today, I'm taking my six-year old to school this morning, and then working on this X-Files project for the rest of the day, followed by dinner with my son and my ex-wife, and then more working on the X-Files story tonight.

If it sounds like this *X-Files* story is kicking my ass all over the place, it is. That's because I want it to be perfect. And because it's kicking my ass, it's holding everything else up. I'm not a big proponent of over-medicating children, and I would loathe to give my child Ritalin (unless there was no other choice), but sometimes I wish I could give it to my muse.

As the deadline clock counts down to Thursday (which is when editor Jonathan Maberry officially sends out a ninja hit squad if I don't turn my story in), I'm agonizing over details like "What name does Skinner call Cigarette Smoking Man by when they're alone in his office?" Which, when you're writing a scene of dialogue between these two characters, is an important detail you'd think someone would have addressed already.

But apparently, in the entire history of the television show, nobody ever has. Does he call him "CSM"? "You black-lunged son of a bitch"? "Boss"? "Spender" (if, indeed, Spender is his real name)?

I'm also debating minutia like "Could Skinner, an Assistant Director at the FBI, legally carry a firearm off-duty with D.C.'s extreme gun laws?" Yeah, might seem trivial, but the answer is the difference between him fighting a were-rat with a handgun versus fighting a were-rat with whatever makeshift weapon he can find in the sewers beneath the city.

Anyway, that's what's on deck for today.

At some point in-between all of that, I will turn forty-seven. Or forty-six. There is some debate over this, but my mother swears it's forty-seven and I feel she ought to know, as she was there.

I don't celebrate my birthday much these days. In truth, I'd forget it was my birthday if not for friends and loved ones who insist on celebrating it for me. And it pleases them to do so, and it pleases me to see them pleased, so it's all good. But I don't really think about birthdays or age anymore. My philosophy—one that I've adopted at this stage in life—is to simply take each day as it comes, good or bad, knowing that another day could follow it, or it could just as easily be my last. That feels me with simultaneous peace and anxiety. Peace because I make sure each day is spent making sure loved ones know what they mean to me, and anxiety because there's still a lot of things left unwritten (although I'm beginning to narrow that gap).

So, that's what I'm doing today. Spending time with the people who are important to me, and working on things that need to be finished.

Just in case.

Because the leaves fall faster.

For the past twenty years, we've watched the writers we grew up reading die—by and large—broke, penniless, poor, without access to proper health insurance or healthcare, without a retirement plan, without savings for a rainy day, and we swore that when we got to that point we'd learn from those mistakes, and we'd find a way to monetize our various IPs so that we didn't have to keep writing new stuff in our golden years, and we wouldn't die in hospices, and our memorials wouldn't be held in retirement homes where the presiding clergy castigates what we wrote for a living, and we wouldn't need to rely on fundraising anthologies put together by our peers and the wholesale liquidation of our archives and estate years before we actually passed.

And now, twenty years later, as the clock comes round, how'd we do with that? How did we fucking do, living from royalty check to royalty check and bill to bill?

Yeah, me neither.

Maybe the next generation will make a better go at it.

Autumn sure came on fast, and I have so far enjoyed the season, but there is so much yet to do and the leaves are coming down faster...

IN HWA "CUNT" IS OKAY, BUT "EMPATHY" IS NOT

I didn't do any Blogging over the weekend, because my son and I were busy with non-writing things. But I'm about to start back again this evening, and thus, I need a little warm-up exercise. Luckily for me, the HWA (Horror Writers Association) was willing to provide the fodder, as they often do.

On Saturday, HWA President Rocky Wood posted a link to a news article on his public Facebook page. The article is about Kerri Rawson, the daughter of the notorious, reprehensible serial killer known as BTK. Rawson, who by all accounts is traumatized and suffering from the aftermath of her father's crimes, has never spoken to the media about the case. Recently, the press contacted her in regards to Stephen King's forthcoming film, *A Good Marriage*, which was partially inspired by the real-life case. Rawson admittedly says some troubling things in the interview, stating that she feels Stephen King is exploiting her family and the victims, and suggesting that it was King's work (and the works of other horror writers) that might have influenced her father's actions. (It has been reported that among the authors BTK read were Stephen King and myself).

No reasonable person is going to agree with Rawson on either point. But it's also fair to say that she might not have the clearest context on this issue. After all, she herself is a victim of her father's crimes. Her entire childhood is a victim. Her memories are victims. With that in mind, perhaps we should feel some empathy and compassion for her, even if we don't agree with her statement.

Instead of showing empathy and compassion, HWA President Rocky Wood called Rawson, quote, "an idiot". Australian author and HWA member Felicity Dowker (posting as Felicity Gray) went further, calling her quote "a cunt". Yet another HWA member made disparaging remarks about Rawson's personal appearance.

When author Nate Southard commented that while Rawson is clearly wrong, maybe the horror professionals in the thread should show a little empathy and not call her "idiot" or "cunt" or disparage her personal appearance, Rocky Wood deleted Nate's comment. Nate was then characterized by Wood as "attacking" Wood and HWA, despite the fact that others, including myself, have since made similar comments.

What's troubling here is President Wood's insistence that his comments (and the comments of other HWA members) don't reflect upon the HWA. This was the same defense used last year when HWA Vice-President Lisa Morton earned the swift ire of Neil Gaiman, Chuck Wendig, John Scalzi, and other professional authors of note (including myself) with <u>her essay on professionalism</u> (a debacle which has been recounted in my non-fiction collection, *Trigger Warnings*).

If you are the President or Vice-President of the Horror Writer's Association, and you comment on something regarding the horror industry, and you make your comment available to the public, then you are representing your organization—the HWA. To suggest otherwise is willful ignorance.

Fellow author Jeff Strand asked me this morning, "Is it

really an HWA controversy if he wasn't speaking on behalf of HWA or on any HWA-related matter?" My response was that it most certainly is. It shouldn't be. But if your President, Vice President, and other assorted members are making such statements publicly, then the public may (rightly or wrongly) see it as such. In this case, as the weekend progressed, it's been deemed as insensitive by many, and has been picked up by media organizations. And thus, it becomes an HWA problem.

I used to be a member of the NRA. I thought NRA Vice-President Wayne LaPierre's comments following some of the tragedies involving gun violence in this country were reprehensible, repugnant, insensitive, and stupid. I didn't vote for him. He didn't speak for me. He didn't speak for a lot of gun owners. Yet his comments were seen by the public as representing the NRA. Therefore, I quit the NRA.

The HWA's officers are public figures. It's ridiculous to say they can't have opinions, but I do think, just like any other public figure, they have to weigh airing those opinions while serving a greater interest (in this case the HWA).

Or, as editor, journalist, and PR specialist Anya Martin put it: "This whole matter of not being able to discuss a bigger issue without name-calling of and lack of empathy towards someone who is clearly a victim to the deletion of comments presenting an alternate point of view is very troubling and rapidly turning into bad PR for HWA."

Again. For the last two decades, it seems like every month brings bad PR for the HWA.

To be clear, I don't disagree that Kerri Rawson is wrong. She's clearly in the wrong. But I agree with Nate Southard, who was characterized as "attacking" Rocky Wood simply by commenting that, while this woman is clearly wrong, maybe we should show a little empathy and not call her "idiot" or "cunt" or disparage her personal appearance.

Your mileage may vary…

UPDATE: Minutes after I posted this, Felicity Dowker/Gray's comments in which the word "cunt" was used were all deleted, apparently by Mr. Wood himself. Perhaps "cunt" isn't okay after all. Or maybe HWA is just getting quicker at damage control...

UPDATE #2: The "idiot" comment has now been edited and changed to "ill-informed".

EBOLA FOR CHRISTMAS

I'm getting over the flu this weekend. If I had a nickel for every person that said, "Maybe you have Ebola", I'd be wealthy. They say it as a joke, of course, but underneath any good joke there is always a truth, and the truth is, people are nervous.

And they should be.

I'm not a fear-monger in real life (although I get paid to be one for my job). I'm not a conspiracy nut. But I am a realist. And realistically, I look at the facts so far, and I get nervous, too.

1. As of this morning, one case of Ebola has been confirmed in Dallas. We've heard of potential cases in Georgia, Utah, Hawaii, Colorado, Virginia, Washington D.C., Kentucky, and Toronto (which is part of North America, so I'm counting it).

There's a chance some of these cases may very well be Ebola. There's also a chance that none of these cases will be Ebola, and instead, will be panicked, frightened people with the flu who are convinced they have Ebola. The longer this goes on, the more frightened, panicked people you have. Enough frightened, panicked people with the flu who think they have Ebola can totally overwhelm our healthcare system, which is still fucked by the way, no matter what either political party tells you.

Overwhelm the hospitals and doctors with frightened, panicked people, and things will get very bad in time for Christmas.

2. The other thing that makes me nervous is the comedy of errors in the response so far, not only from Dallas authorities, but from the CDC, DHS, and other federal organizations. We've all seen the news footage of the crew pressure washing the victim's highly-infected vomit off the sidewalk while not wearing any protective gear whatsoever. We know that he was misdiagnosed by the hospital, and sent back home to possibly infect more. We know that one of the people he possibly infected took a trip to Walmart to buy a blanket. We know that the ambulance he was transported in and the EMS professionals who were with him weren't taken out of circulation until almost 48 hours later. We know that last night, the mayor of Dallas asked everybody to go to block parties and fish fries and football games (oddly echoing the mayor of Amity in *Jaws*, with his insistence that everyone go to the beach, despite the fact that a shark had killed somebody).

I can excuse the local Texas authorities. Local municipalities are seldom prepared for things on this potential scale of magnitude. They relied on information and orders from the CDC, DHS, and other federal agencies—all of whom have once again dropped the ball.

What really concerns me is the number of people who watch the CDC response, and nod their heads enthusiastically, and repeat, "We can handle this. We are not Liberia. Our government is equipped to deal with this." Because that's simply not true. They bungled their response on 9/11. They bungled their response to Hurricane Katrina. They bungled their response to the financial meltdown and the bank bailout. They bungled their response to Benghazi. They've bungled their response to Ferguson. And they will bungle their response to this new crisis. That's because we are relying on bureaucracy. We're not talking about your favorite political party or favorite President. This has nothing to do with Democrats or Republicans, Liberals or Conservatives, Bush or Obama. Bureaucracy exists beyond those parameters. Bureaucracy is a slow, lumbering, stupid beast, and it cannot respond swiftly.

Don't expect bureaucracy to keep you safe from Ebola, or any other crisis. Responsibility for your safety and the safety of those you care about, begins and ends with you. Country boys like myself have always known this. These days, trendy folks call that "prepping" and there are TV shows about it, and I get to teach my city friends how to can green beans the way my Grandma did, and run a trout line the way my Grandpa did, and skin a buck the way my father did. You can call it prepping if you like. We always just called it a part of life.

Education and self-reliance will beat panic and bureaucratic incompetence every time.

If you disagree with me, that's cool. It's okay. But this Ebola thing? It's not going away anytime soon. And at some point this winter, you or a family member are going to catch the flu. And at some point during that, you're going to feel a twist in your gut, and you're going to wonder…is it just the flu?

All I want for Christmas is for people to start thinking for themselves and taking care of each other, rather than letting bureaucracy do both.

MORE ON BTK AND HWA

Last week, I wrote about the repugnant responses made by various HWA members, including their President, in regards to an interview with the daughter of the notorious BTK serial killer, in which she criticized Stephen King.

The reporter of the original news story, Roy Wenzel, contacted me last week for a follow-up piece about the controversy. And although I am quoted extensively (and fairly) in the article, I had the flu at the time, and didn't turn the rest of my interview questions in in time for publication. But I think they're pretty good answers, especially given that they were written under the influence of NyQuil, so I'm reproducing them here for posterity.

On what Kerri Rawson said about King's BTK-related work:

Well, I think she's speaking from a place of unimaginable pain and sorrow, and I'm sympathetic to that. I make my living imagining what other people are going through, but I cannot fathom what it must be like for her. I feel for her. But, that being said, as a creator, I obviously disagree with her comments. They are her opinion, but it's an opinion I disagree with.

On why some people blame the horror genre after a tragedy.

It's foolish—and dangerous—to blame an artist or an artist's work. And yes, even though video games and horror novels are mass-produced entertainment, they're still art and they're still produced by artists. Should Trent Reznor of Nine Inch Nails or Celine Dion be held responsible if someone suffering from depression and a broken heart reacts badly to one of their songs? Should filmmakers take the blame if an unstable individual identifies with the wrong elements of *Taxi Driver* or *Dexter*?

I grew up reading Stephen King. And he's been gracious enough to give me some support. And sure, he's had an influence on me, but only in that I also make my living writing horror novels. I had friends who grew up reading Stephen King. They went on to become a doctor, a mechanic, a tech support worker, and a foundry supervisor. And another one went to jail. In all of their cases, I don't think *'Salem's Lot* or *The Stand* pushed them one way or the other.

These are works of fiction. They are meant to entertain. They are meant to get you through your lunch break or study hall or your long commute home. They're to keep you company at night, or to provide a temporary distraction from whatever you have going on in life. Some people have a bizarre emotional reaction to *The Catcher in the Rye*, but we don't blame J.D. Salinger for that.

On why people enjoy the horror genre.

I think there's a safety in it. There's a safety in fictional monsters. In real life, there are monsters flying airplanes into skyscrapers and abducting children and embezzling retirement funds. And there seems to be more of them all the time. Fictional monsters provide a release from all that.

On why I took a stand against the HWA members and their comments.

I can't stand bullying, and what I saw—from my perspective—was a young woman being bullied. No, I don't agree with what she said, but like I said before, it comes from a place of unimaginable pain, and I think the name-calling and derision of her by people who are supposed to be professionals in this field was just as wrong. There's too much ugliness in the world. As writers—especially writers of horror fiction—we should be looking for beauty and truth and compassion instead.

So, there you have it. Roy tells me that the BTK Killer himself has also commented on this controversy, and the statements made by Rocky Wood, Stephen King, and myself. You can read more about that in Roy's latest article.

And yes, it bothers me that the BTK Killer reads Brian Keene novels. But I don't reckon there is anything I can do about it. Not every reader is going to be a stalwart member of society. Some of them will, in fact, be assholes.

But not you. Or you. Or you two over there in the corner. You, I like.

A CAPTAIN MARVEL FOR EVERY GENERATION

On Saturday, my six-year old son and I were watching an episode of *Batman: The Brave and the Bold* guest-starring DC's version of Captain Marvel. When Batman referred to the character by that name, my son asked, "Why do they keep calling him that? His name is Shazam."

"No," I replied. "Shazam is just the magic word he uses to transform. His real name is Captain Marvel."

"Don't be silly, Dad," my son said. "Everyone knows that Captain Marvel is a girl."

He was referring, of course, to Marvel's current incarnation of the character, penned by Kelly Sue DeConnick, in which Carol Danvers (formerly Ms. Marvel) is now known as Captain Marvel. He's six years old. He's grown up with this version of the character. He's seen her on *Super Hero Squad* and *The Avengers* cartoon and in the comic books we buy and read together. He knows about Mar-vell, the Seventies version of the character, but for him, Captain Marvel is a woman. And always will be.

And I think that's awesome.

That's why I was never a fan of Marvel's sliding time-scale.

Oh, I understand brands and trademarks, and intellectual property (I own all three myself). But I would have loved it if Peter Parker had grown up with me. I would have loved it if the awkward teenager I read about as an awkward teenager, had gone through his thirties and forties with me, and perhaps helped guide a new, generational Spider-Man, such as Miles Morales or May Parker. Imagine a Spider-Man where all of that continuity does more than just "count"—it informs a now fifty-year old Peter Parker, as he uses it to be an Uncle Ben to a young Miles Morales, teaching him the lessons that Parker himself learned the hard way.

And this could easily be done while maintaining the brand and IP. Mar-vell is no longer Captain Marvel, but the brand and IP still exist, and an entire generation (at least those who read comics) is growing up knowing that "Captain Marvel is a girl".

The greatest roadblock to storytelling in the comic book medium isn't continuity. It's the insistence (by both fans and editors) on the illusion of change.

Every generation deserves their own Captain Marvel.

FEAR OF AN OLD PLANET

Yesterday evening, I pull in to a convenience store to get gas. I've got Public Enemy's *Apocalypse 91* booming from the car stereo. *Apocalypse 91*, by the way, comes in at #2 on my list of the Top Ten Greatest Hip-Hop Albums of All Time (sandwiched in-between Dr. Dre's *The Chronic* at #1 and Ice-T's *Home Invasion* at #3).

But I digress. Anyway, I get out of the car and proceed to gas up. My radio is still playing. I notice a group of teenagers loitering and watching me. They look like one of those multicultural street gangs that only existed in Seventies movies or Eighties Marvel Comics. This makes me happy. When I was a teenager, I also loitered in this particular store's parking lot from time to time, and back then, you never saw black kids, white kids, and brown kids hanging out together like that. It's yet another little reminder of how diversity has come to rural Central Pennsylvania.

One of them nods at me and asks, "What is that?"

"An Oldsmobile Aurora," I say, thinking he means the car.

"No, the music. What's that music?"

"That's Public Enemy."

"It sounds…different."

I shrug. "This is what rap used to sound like, back when it was about things other than how much money you got, and who is guest-starring on your song."

He blinks at me.

"I like the beat," one of his friends says.

"Listen to the lyrics," I advise. "They mean something. Listen close."

From the car, Chuck D says, "You never know if you only trust the TV and the radio. These days you can't see who's in cahoots, cause now the KKK's wearing three-piece suits…"

The kids then ask me what year the song was recorded. When I tell them, they grin.

One of them says, "Damn, that shit is old. I'm gonna see if my Moms has it at home."

I drive away, feeling a strange simultaneous mix of bemusement, hope for the future, and of getting very, very old.

Speaking of getting older, here's something else I've been thinking about recently.

As a kid, growing up in the late-Seventies and early-Eighties, I had an awesome collection of record albums and comic books. Eventually, the albums were replaced with cassette tapes and then compact discs, and ultimately digital files. The comic books were replaced with collected editions (such as the Marvel Essential trade paperbacks) or archival hardcovers (such as The Spirit Archives and the Complete EC Collection).

This has cost a lot of money over the years.

Now, I find myself slowly returning to my roots. I've been slowly buying vinyl again, because quite frankly, as I age, it sounds better to me than a digital file. So far, I've limited myself mostly to essential, desert island, must-have albums.

I'm seriously contemplating doing the same with comic books. At one time, I had a complete run of *The Defenders*. Now, I have a complete run of Marvel's archival series of *The Defenders*. But the reproductions in those collected editions leaves something to be desired, and I miss viewing the covers and the advertisements and the Bullpen Bulletins. I had a complete run of *Kamandi: The Last Boy on Earth*. Now I have an incomplete run of the hardcover DC Archives *Kamandi: The Last Boy on Earth*, because DC decided to stop producing those before completely reprinting the entire series.

Comic retailers seem to agree that the market for back issues has really declined in recent years. I have to wonder if it might see an upswing again in coming years, as more collectors my age decide that the originals were better?

GOING TO EXTREMES: SOME THOUGHTS ON EXTREME HORROR

Recently, it has become a trendy thing to decry the extreme horror sub-genre.

I've never been one for tribalism or nationalism or any sort of team spirit. That's probably why I was never much of a sports fan. Oh, I enjoy going out in the backyard and playing football with friends or engaging in a friendly sparring match, but I absolutely loathe watching professional sports. I'm not one to root for a team and shower hate and derision on another group simply because they are from a different team. Giants or Jets. Orioles or Yankees. Coke or Pepsi. Marvel or DC. Left or Right. Progressive or Conservative. FOX or MSNBC. Muslin or Jew. Christian or Atheist. Catholic or Protestant. Star Wars or Star Trek. The Beatles or the Rolling Stones. You must choose. Pick one.

Fuck you.

I choose not to choose. You go ahead and stick to your favorite team. You continue shouting at each other until everything comes to a screeching halt. Keep building walls around your individual fiefdoms and refuse to consider the other side's views. Let the ever-increasing xenophobia and tribalism that is fucking this world up continue to roll on unchecked. While you're doing all that, I'll be over here in the corner, carving out a safe-house for the last true Independents and Individualists.

I have always applied that same aesthetic to my reading and writing. I've been reading horror (as a genre) since I was six years old, and I've been writing it professionally since I was in my mid-thirties. I enjoy reading all of the various spectrums and sub-genres—quiet, supernatural, extreme, splatterpunk, surreal, bizarro, cosmic, new weird, old weird, pulp, grindhouse, comedic, etc.—and I think it's wonderful that our field has such a wide and ranging palate. Extreme horror is a valid and vital part of that rich tapestry, but too often, it is met with derision and dismissal from some who don't even understand what it is they are criticizing.

To announce that a particular literary styling or genre trapping is not to your individual taste is perfectly acceptable. Personally, I don't care for most post-Anne Rice vampire fiction. It's not my bag, but I'm perfectly fine with other people reading and writing it. I expect the same mutual courtesy when it comes to extreme horror. Dismissing it under the blanket condemnation of "it's nothing but buckets of blood and cum" or decrying its readers and writers and fans as "degenerates" does nothing but show the ignorance of the critic in question.

Extreme horror, when done correctly, can evoke a range of emotions—from the comedic (selected works of Edward Lee, Ryan Harding, and Shane McKenzie), to the poetic (Monica J. O'Rourke, Charlee Jacob, and Wrath James White), to the hauntingly transcendent (Jack Ketchum's *The Girl Next Door*, Nate Southard's *Just Like Hell*, and J. F. Gonzalez's *Survivor*).

The important part of that is "when done correctly." Because, yes, when done incorrectly, extreme horror is nothing but what its opponents say it is—buckets of blood and cum with no intrinsic value and cardboard characters that exist only to be butchered. However, when done correctly, extreme horror can be one of the most effective branches of our genre.

J. F. Gonzalez's *Survivor*, for example, is a brutal and unflinching narrative of a pregnant young mother who has been kidnapped by a snuff film ring. The prose is harrowing, and does not shirk in describing the atrocities she witnesses and the things she does to survive. But it also has moments of beauty and truth, such as *"Go forth and do what I will not be able to do. Live life. Enjoy life. And more importantly, appreciate the beauty in life. Do this for me."* You don't get a sentence like that—and get the reader to feel the emotional impact of a sentence like that—without first creating a character that the reader can empathize with, and then putting that character through the proverbial ringer. Gonzalez did this masterfully. *Survivor* is often cited (along with Ketchum's *The Girl Next Door*) as one of the best extreme horror novels of all time. And rightfully so, because it is.

Survivor is a wonderful novel, regardless of genre. But it is also a horror novel. The purpose of a horror novel is to evoke feelings of fear and dread in the reader. Gonzalez could have written *Survivor* in the quiet style of the masterful Ramsey Campbell or Charles L. Grant. He could have invoked the cosmic moodiness of Thomas Ligotti or Laird Barron. He could have gone for the Americana pop-culture formula of Stephen King or Dean Koontz. He could have written it in any of those styles and it would have still been a perfectly serviceable, perfectly readable horror novel. However, this is a novel about a pregnant woman who is kidnapped by a snuff film ring. To truly serve that plot (and the reader) he wrote it as an extreme horror novel, and because of that, *Survivor* goes from serviceable and readable to unforgettable and seminal.

Remember, a horror novel is supposed to evoke fear and dread in the reader. *Survivor* does so, in spades. The reason for this is because the extreme nature serves the story.

The same could be said of another seminal extreme horror novel, Jack Ketchum's *The Girl Next Door*. In his famous speech at the 1998 Bram Stoker Awards, author Douglas E. Winter stated, "Horror is not a genre. It is an emotion." Never has this been more apt than when it comes to discussing *The Girl Next Door*.

In a year when readers could choose between the traditional, literary, suggestively quiet horror typified by Grant, Klein, or Straub, and the artfully-gory, hyper-intensive limitless horror of the splatterpunks, Jack Ketchum's *The Girl Next Door* arrived with (perhaps unknowingly) a middle finger extended to both of those camps. It eschewed genre subcategories while simultaneously straddling them. The prose was lean when it needed to be (think Richard Laymon by way of Charles Bukowski or Ernest Hemingway), and more expansive and literary when the narrative called for it. There were quiet, heartfelt, descriptive moments (especially at the beginning when protagonist David is introducing the reader to the town and the cast and what life is like for them) but these then give way to some of the most soul-rending physical and sexual atrocities ever committed to the printed page.

Because of the latter, some critics labeled *The Girl Next Door* as a new splatterpunk novel, but it wasn't. While it certainly contained enough violence and blood to qualify as such, it differed on an emotional level from the standard splatterpunk fare. Until that point, even the most exceptional splatterpunk novel (and there were many) had been about art. Splatterpunk's stated intention was that of the court jester, utilizing graphic, extremely gory prose to, as Phillip Nutman put it, "reflect the moral chaos of our times." And while splatterpunk certainly succeeded with blood red colors at doing this, the artistic aspect was always prevalent, and thus, the reader's emotional attachment to the work was often subdued. The best splatterpunk novels were like pretty paintings on the walls. You marveled at their beauty, but you couldn't walk inside the painting and feel them. The same went for the other side of the genre. The quiet, traditional horror, while quite lovely to read, too often felt detached, and hard to connect with emotionally.

Emotion—primal emotion—was what had been missing from much of Eighties' horror fiction, and *The Girl Next Door* brought it. The novel went places that horror fiction simply wasn't supposed to go to, but not just through the physical violence depicted therein. No. It evoked an emotional response in readers that horror fiction had long been lacking. If splatterpunk did indeed reflect humanity's moral chaos, then *The Girl Next Door* was a mirror image of its pathos and sheer nihilism.

It was horror, pushed to the extremes.

The Girl Next Door defied every subcategory that existed within the horror genre, and in doing so, set itself apart as something new. Something different. It wasn't a novel painted in black and white, but in murky shades of gray. And red. There were no good guys. No last minute reprieves. No happy endings. *The Girl Next Door* didn't just break down storytelling tropes and genre expectations—it gutted them in a basement bomb shelter and left them bleeding out on the floor. And in the process, it left many readers feeling the same way.

It left them feeling.

It left them feeling uncomfortable. It left them feeling fear and dread.

It pushed them to the extremes, because that is what the story called for.

I've written some extreme horror novels. *The Rising, City of the Dead, Castaways, Urban Gothic, Jack's Magic Beans, Dead Sea*, and *Entombed* immediately come to mind. In each case, I did so because that's what the story demanded. But I've also written other types of horror, including all of the various sub-categories I mentioned earlier. And yet, despite having produced works that are firmly quiet or cosmic or supernatural, I am best known as an extreme horror writer.

And I'm okay with that. Because I am.

One of the most extreme things I've ever written isn't even classified by readers as extreme. In the second chapter of my novel *Dark Hollow*, the protagonist reflects on a miscarriage his wife suffered earlier that year, and how it impacted them both emotionally. This scene is not gory, but it is unflinching in its emotional honesty, and in all the years that book has been in print, it seems to be the one that readers bring up the most. They tell me I took them to emotional extremes with that scene. That I made them feel.

Which is my job. And if I have to go to extremes to successfully do my job, then I will.

As long as it serves the story you are trying to tell, never apologize for writing extreme horror. And if it makes you feel something and shows you a truth, never apologize for reading it either.

As I write this, the Ebola pandemic is still in the news. So are warnings that terrorists are crossing the Mexican border, while war-hawks bellow for a full-scare war with Russia in the Ukraine. An increasingly militarized police force has trampled Constitutional rights in Boston, then the Bundy ranch, and now Ferguson. Protesting turns to looting, and buildings burn while rage seethes. Recently, a senior minister in India's government downplayed a horrendous attack in which a young woman was gang-raped to death on a city bus as, quote, "a small incident". Not too long ago, a police officer in Ferguson, Missouri derisively told an African-American woman named Lillian Guthrie to, quote, "Get a job." Lillian is a successful financial analyst. While you were sleeping, soldiers of the Islamic State massacred the Iraqi village of Kocho. After slaughtering every adult male, they transported the women and children to the city of Tal Afar. There, the male children will be pressed into becoming fighters for the group. The women and female children will be forced into sexual slavery or sold on the black market for the same. For the past several months, the Boko Haram group has been doing the same thing all across Nigeria, abducting young women and little girls, with the intent of a similar fate.

In light of all that, Edward Lee's recurring characters, Dickie and Balls, don't seem so bad. Indeed, they seem like two fellows whom I might like to curl up with for an evening, just to escape the very real atrocities happening all around me. Because no matter what depravity Edward Lee has them engage in (and Lord knows there has been quite the gamut of it) he always does so with a wink and a nod. That's his style, and it's one that serves his extreme fiction well. You can always hear him snickering behind the pages. And we, as readers, can't help but chuckle along.

The world is going to extremes.

Why should we be any different?

A NEW AGE OF FUCKERY

There is a justified uproar about the business practices of Permuted Press taking place right now. In a nutshell, they are refusing to revert rights to their authors, despite the books not being in print. You can read all about it via the Blogs of Graeme Reynolds, Gabrielle Faust, and R. Thomas Riley, and Jack Hanson (four newer authors whom I have an immense amount of respect for) and William Miekle (who's been at this I think as long as I have and knows the score).

Authors have privately been asking me to look into this over the last few weeks, and although I've been dealing with my best friend's alarming health diagnosis, and an alarming health diagnosis of my own, and deadlines, and the everyday adventures of being the parent of a six-year old, I have. I have looked into it and it is abhorrent. It is not, however, illegal.

Permuted Press should, on good faith to the community and to their stable of writers, revert those print rights back to the individual authors. That would be the right and moral thing to do. However, corporations seldom do the right or moral thing, especially when Intellectual Property is involved, and especially when that Intellectual Property can be strip-mined for film, comic books, television, merchandising, etc. And in the case of Permuted, they have no legal obligation to do the right or moral thing. Indeed. their legal obligation is to hold on to those rights, because as I understand it, the contracts their authors signed state that they can.

As I said on author Laird Barron's Facebook page this morning, Permuted Press has been dodgy since day one. I did an Afterword for one of their very early anthologies, got a glimpse at their contracts then, and stayed far, far away. A decade plus later, nothing much seems to have changed, despite new owners.

But it's also important to note that, unlike Dorchester/Leisure, it doesn't sound as if Permuted is doing anything 'illegal'. Dodgy? Yes. Shifty as fuck? Yes. But from what sources have told me, they are going by contractual terms, and if the authors signed those contracts with those terms, then that's not illegal.

Laird is absolutely right. You need to understand what you are signing and what it means for your Intellectual Property. Take a community college business course (like I did), come from a business background, or get an agent (or ideally, all three). In this age, Intellectual Property is king, and the advent of digital means your IP can stay in print in perpetuity, and make other people a lot of money—unless you've got control of it."

Let me be clear. I stand firmly with the authors in this fight, and I will personally boycott purchasing all Permuted Press titles until the company does the morally right thing (and I applaud you if you do the same) and reverts those print rights to their authors.

But we are going to see more and more and more stories like this, and at some point, boycotts and Blogs aren't going to be enough.

In the aftermath of Dorchester and others, and with the advent of respectable, responsible self-publishing via digital, and with the headline-grabbing stories of Intellectual Property battles in comic book and Young Adult publishing, there is absolutely no excuse for authors not managing control over their rights and their IP. The days of simply writing the books and letting others control the paperwork are gone. As an author, it is your responsibility to shepherd your Intellectual Property.

1. Never, ever publish without a contract.

2. Never, ever sign a contract unless you understand it. If you are using an agent, make that agent explain the parts you don't understand. If the agent doesn't want to explain it, get a new agent.

3. Never, ever sign a contract you're not comfortable with just because you are excited to be published or to be working with that publisher.

4. Never, ever give away the rights to anything. Make sure you are paid for them. If you are dealing with a book publisher, why would you give them your movie rights? Are they making movies, or are they publishing books? Never assume those rights won't be used. For twenty years, I've retained the rights to things like apparel, toys, etc. for my books. Those rights were never used by anyone, yet I made sure I retained them. Now, there is a successful line of t-shirts based on my books being produced by a vendor. Had I not held on to those rights, I would have had to either split those monies with my publishers, or not made a cent off them at all.

You can't just be a writer these days. I'm sorry. I know that's not romantic. But it's true. In addition to being a writer, you have to be a salesperson and a marketer and an agent and a lawyer. Or else you need to hire one of each and have them on your team.

Most importantly, you need to remember that quite often,

your peers and readers will also be on your team. if you do get screwed, then you need to do as Graeme, Gabrielle, Jack, Willie, and R. Thomas have done above. You have the right (and I personally believe an obligation) to speak out publicly, stating the facts and letting the public decide.

SOLIDARITY ISN'T JUST FOR UNIONS

Yesterday, I linked to a number of Blogs and reports from other authors detailing alarming allegations about Permuted Press. I stated that, based on the evidence presented, I would be joining those authors (as a consumer) in boycotting the publisher until it did the right thing by all its authors. Throughout the day, more former and current Permuted Press authors offered their own thoughts, many of which echoed the complaints of the original posters.

A handful of current Permuted Press authors, however, took issue with my Blog entry. Their rebuttals varied from "Gabrielle Faust is lying" to "At least when Permuted Press fucks you, they buy you dinner first!" In the case of the former, the individuals in question did not respond when it was pointed out to them that other authors were reporting similar allegations independently of Gabrielle Faust. And I don't think I even need to point out the lunacy in the "Well yeah, they fucked us but they bought us lunch first" defense.

One thing I saw echoed was a concern that, yes, while a number of authors did apparently get screwed, not everyone did, and a boycott was unfair to those authors who were still with the company, as it would impact their bottom line.

"We're sorry some of our peers got screwed," was the theme of the refrain, "but we're still here. What can we do about it? All a boycott will do is impact our own personal bottom line."

Which is fair. Yes, a consumer boycott does impact them. But so does a publisher refusing to release the print rights of their peers. Any time a publisher does anything to an author, it impacts all authors, because it sets a precedent.

What impacts one author impacts us all.

During the respective falls of both Dorchester Publishing and Night Shade Books, you saw authors from outside those respective stables standing in solidarity with the authors directly affected. More importantly, you saw authors WHO WERE STILL WITH DORCHESTER AND NIGHT SHADE urging Dorchester and Night Shade to do the right thing.

Why? Because what impacts one author impacts us all.

A young author asked me recently why I was so interested in the fight between Hatchette and Amazon, since I'm not published by Hatchette. I explained the big picture to her, demonstrating that the outcome of that decision will impact us all, no matter which way it plays out. You cannot be a professional author and NOT have a stake or interest in that fight.

What impacts one author impacts us all.

Publicly, it's no secret that there's no love lost these days between myself and the HWA. But earlier this year, when there was some behind the scenes nonsense concerning my receiving the Grandmaster Award—the organizers of that year's World Horror Convention orchestrated an attempt to block me from being there to receive the award—some HWA officers privately stepped into the fight, on my side. And those officers know I would do the same for them, regardless of our disagreements. Why? Not because I'm going to run for office in the organization. But because what impacts one author impacts us all.

Personally, I am not a fan of some of the things said over the years by Vox Day (Theodore Beale). Indeed, I find Vox Day to be loathsome, racist, homophobic, and misogynistic. He's a scum-fuck. But if he was getting screwed by a publisher, I'd speak up about it. Why? Not because I agree with his personal views or the things he says online. Not because I'm anxious to play out some gender role or score points with a particular political group. But because what impacts one author impacts us all.

So, if you're still with Permuted Press, what can you do? Well, instead of shooting the messengers, you can go to your publisher, privately or publicly, and say, "Look. I'm very happy with you. But we're getting an awful lot of bad press, and it is personally impacting my bottom line. Will you please consider reverting these print rights, or at least addressing everyone's concerns in a prompt, responsible, and public fashion?"

And if they don't—if they refuse—then ask yourself if they are really concerned about your own bottom line.

Because what impacts one author impacts us all.

Now, I've written about this for two days, and feel I've clearly communicated my thoughts and where I stand on the issue. If anyone, on either side, wants to continue to argue or misconstrue what I said, they'll have to do so without my participation. I've got other stuff to take care of. As I said, a friend of mine is very sick, and there are things more important than this shit. You kids need to learn to start fighting your own battles, because I'm not always going to be here to do it for you.

1 OPPRESSION

I woke at three o'clock this morning, unable to sleep because I've got a ton of stuff on my mind, and for once, none of it is work-related. After I figured out I wasn't going back to sleep, I decided to work instead.

I turned on Ken Burns' wonderful Civil War documentary for background noise, and was struck by this quote from Abraham Lincoln: *"As a nation, we began by declaring that 'all men are created equal.' We now practically read it 'all men are created equal, except negroes.' When the Know-Nothings get control, it will read 'all men are created equal, except negroes, and foreigners, and Catholics.' When it comes to this I should prefer emigrating to some country where they make no pretense of loving liberty; to Russia, for instance, where despotism can be taken pure, and without the base alloy of hypocrisy."*

I propose that now, in 2014, it should read 'all men are created equal, except young Black men guilty of walking down the street, elderly white men grazing their cattle on land that has belonged to their ranch for generations, women who write video game reviews, gay men and gay women who want to get married, Muslims who go out in public dressed as a

Muslim, anyone who legally owns a firearm, anyone who goes through airport security, anyone driving a car, anyone using a computer or phone or other electronic device, anyone who happens to cross paths with a police officer, anyone who is not a banker or a politician or part of the 1%, and any man, woman, or child who lives in America today. We are your overlords. Here. Play *Angry Birds* and look at cat memes and watch *Project Runway* and the five-hundred billion superhero movies Hollywood is cranking out. Pay no attention to what we're doing.'

That's what it should read.

THE SECRET TO CRAFTING EFFECTIVE HORROR

Late last night, award-winning game developer Guido Henkel, writer Anthony Trevino, and myself were discussing the latest *Godzilla* remake, which I hated. I compared it to the pictures of food on the menu at McDonalds—they look nice, but they have no substance and ultimately, once you get the food, it doesn't live up to what is pictured on the menu. In a nutshell, that's the new *Godzilla* remake for me.

Anyway, Guido brought up a great point when he asked, "Why would you want to care for the characters? It's a Godzilla movie."

Godzilla films have never scared me. I love them, and both *Destroy All Monsters* and *Final Wars* turn me into fan-boy goo, but I have never found them scary. By contrast, the original black and white *King Kong* scares me to this day (it is absolutely my favorite giant monster movie of all time). What's the difference between them? I'll explain in a moment.

This latest *Godzilla* remake was billed as scary. The filmmakers, in interviews, stated that their intent was to scare the audience. The marketing campaign advertised it as a scary horror film. Why then, did it fail where the original black and white *King Kong* succeeded?

Because of its characters. *King Kong* took the time to develop a wide variety of characters whom I grew to care about. Even the minor crewmen from the ship had personalities of their own. The characters in the new *Godzilla* (with the exception of Bryan Cranston) are wooden, one-dimensional, and motivated by seemingly nothing other than the script.

The key to crafting effective horror—be it prose, film, video games, or comics—is to create characters that the audience can empathize and sympathize with. If you're going to do something scary to the character—be it having them chased through the woods by a maniac with a chainsaw or menaced by a forty-story tall radioactive monster—then you must first establish an emotional connection between them and the audience.

It's the difference between Eli Roth's *Hostel* and Jack Ketchum's *The Girl Next Door*. Both works feature soul-numbing atrocities, but the former fails, because we simply do not care about the characters, while the latter triumphs, because we care too much.

You want to scare your audience? Start with a character they can believe in. One that perhaps reminds them of themselves a bit. One they can identify with and feel for. Once you've established that bond, make bad things happen to them.

That's how you create horror, especially for today's jaded, "seen-it-all" audience, who—if you don't hold their attention—will get distracted by Facebook or Twitter or Angry Birds halfway through your efforts.

Which is why, halfway through the new *Godzilla*, I started playing Words with Friends and didn't look up from my phone again.

ON WASTING VOTES

I will vote today, as I've done in every election since turning eighteen. My choices this time around will either be the Libertarian Party or the Green Party, depending on whether or not those two parties have a candidate available on my state's ballot.

Once finished, I will leave the polling station. And, as invariably happens in this rural two-party stronghold, some well-meaning person will ask me if I voted Democratic or Republican, and I will explain that I voted for neither, because neither of those parties meet the requirements of my own moral and ethical code. And then that well-meaning person will tell me that I wasted my vote.

And I will once again refrain from punching them in the face.

My Dad and I had a similar discussion years ago. He was frustrated with my choices (that year, I was deciding between voting for the Socialist candidate or the Libertarian candidate), and he said: "You served your country. I served my country. Your Grandfather and Great-Grandfather and Great-Uncle served their country. Why would you waste your vote? That's what we fought for."

My initial response was that none of us fought specifically for that right to vote. I served my country because I couldn't get into college and couldn't find a job. My father served his country because our government decided that Vietnam shouldn't fall to Communists. My Grandfather and Great-Uncle served their country because Germany and the Japanese declared war on us. And my Great-Grandfather—well, when he was gassed in that trench during World War One (an event which literally turned his hair white), I'm pretty fucking sure voting wasn't on his mind.

I bit down on this response, because my Dad is in his Seventies and set in his ways, and also because in theory, he's right. Voting is something that is supposed to be guaranteed to all American citizens, and yes, had the Germans or the Japanese or the NVC taken over this country, I suppose it is a right we would have lost.

Why, then, is there not more outrage from Americans regarding how futile that right—the right to vote—has become? Those of us who vote for third parties do so primarily because we feel that the Democrats and Republicans are two sides of the same coin, beholden to special interests and lobbyists, offering no real change. We feel they are groups who do not represent our own personal, moral, political, ethical views and concerns. We feel that voting for them would be a wasted vote. And so, we vote Libertarian, Socialist, Green, Constitutional, and all the other viable third-party choices that we are given.

And every year, we are mocked and derided for participating in our patriotic duty, told that we are wasting *our* vote by people who we feel just wasted *their* vote.

The truth is, the only wasted vote is a vote not cast.

And truthfully, I'm starting to suspect that not voting might not be a wasted effort, either.

PEOPLE ARE PEOPLE

When my novel *Dead Sea* first came out many years ago, dozens of critics and reviewers made a big deal out of the book's main protagonist being a gay black man. They made an even bigger deal out of the fact that a straight white guy had written it.

Now, don't get me wrong. I'm not complaining. Those reviews were universally kind and enthusiastic. They celebrated the fact that it was a diverse horror novel. But what left me bemused (and still does) was their questions. Why did I go with a non-white, non-straight hero? What was I trying to say? And how did I make him so authentic? How did I get inside his head?

My answer was always the same: my readership is estimated at somewhere between fifty-thousand to one hundred thousand people (depending on the availability of the book, price point, and other factors). Not all of those readers are straight white males. Not all of my friends are straight white males. Not all of my peers are straight white males. And not all of the world is straight white males.

I have no agenda, other than creating realistic characters that people can identify with, feel for, and believe. Those three elements are crucial for any type of character-driven fiction, but they are absolutely essential for horror fiction. My only goal has always been to create characters that my audience can identify with, no matter what color, gender, religion, or sexual orientation.

One of the novel's I'm working on right now, called *The Complex*, has a main protagonist who is trans. I'm sure when it comes out, the critics and reviewers will ask those questions again. Why did I make the hero trans? What was I trying to say? How did I get into their head and make them so believable?

And my answer will be the same.

People are people. When you get past the dogma and affiliations that divide us on the surface, deep inside we all have the same hopes and fears. Hope and fear are the two things that drive horror fiction.

People are people so why shouldn't fictional people be representative of the same? There doesn't have to be an agenda. It doesn't have to be shoehorned in. There should never be a soapbox (at least in escapist fiction). But a writer can and should do their best to reflect the world around them. And there are all kinds of people in this world.

ON LITERARY ESTATES

I've written before (in *Trigger Warnings* and elsewhere) about the importance of establishing a literary estate, but I'd like to expand upon that this morning because it's been on my mind these past few weeks.

If you are a writer, you need some form of legal document outlining your affairs in the event of your death. It doesn't matter if you are an unpublished beginner or an old pro with forty paperback novels to your name.

It should provide answers to the following:

1. Who controls the rights to your published and unpublished works (print, foreign, film, etc.) in the event of your death.
2. Who receives the royalties, advances, and other monetary sums for those works, and who future checks should be made out to in the event of your death.
3. Who controls and has access to your media presence (your website, Facebook page, Twitter, etc.) in the event of your death.

4. What should be done with any unfinished works in the event of your death.
5. Your passwords and log-in information for your computer, your email, your websites, and most-importantly (if you are self-publishing via Kindle, Nook, or Kobo) your log-in information for your self-published material in the event of your death.

Ideally, you'll have a lawyer draw this up. But if you can't afford that, there are still things you can do. Neil Gaiman has some sound advice on his website (including a helpful PDF template to make your own document). You can also type everything up, go to your local notary, pay forty dollars to get it notarized with a witness, and put that among your important papers.

You also need to make sure that whomever is in charge of your literary estate is aware of their involvement. Communicate to them the things you expect of them, in the event of your death. In my office, there is a sealed envelope marked 'IN CASE OF EMERGENCY: BREAK GLASS'. It contains the documents outlining my literary estate, as well as all my passwords, log-in information, and other important things my heirs will need to benefit from my work after I am gone. Two people—my second ex-wife and author J.F. Gonzalez—know where this envelope is located. It stays hidden every day, sitting there unneeded.

Until one day when it will be needed.

But that's not something I'll need to worry about, and when that day comes, neither will my family and heirs.

If you are a writer, and you don't have a literary estate set up, I urge you to do so as soon as possible. Instead of working on your novel, story, script, etc. today, take a few hours to work on this instead.

Your loved ones will thank you when the time comes, and you don't know when that time will be.

We never know when that time will be.
The leaves are falling faster...

MATTERS OF PERSPECTIVE

Yesterday, I received a royalty check from Marvel Comics for $11.40 (digital sales for *Dead of Night: Devil-Slayer*, which more of you obviously need to purchase).

My six-year old thought the check was pretty neat, although he was disappointed that there wasn't a picture of Spider-Man on it. (There used to be one on their checks, but that's been done away with since they were purchased by Walt Disney. Perhaps it's yet another example of the notorious penny-pinching by owner Ike Perlmutter).

Anyway...$11.40 for a comic book, which will be deposited in my bank account on Monday, and which my son and I will then spend on more comic books (his pull list right now includes *Teen Titans Go, Tiny Titans, Captain Action Cat, Scooby-Doo Team-Up,* and other all-ages books). And thus, the comics circle of life comes round again...

Speaking of comic books and superheroes, when I was a kid, we had *The Incredible Hulk, Spider-Man, Wonder Woman, Flash,* and *Captain America* television shows (and a *Dr. Strange* made-for-TV movie). We had the Christopher Reeve *Superman* movies. A few years later, we had Tim Burton's *Batman*.

And then the market for superhero-based properties dried up, because viewers got tired of them all, and tuned in to other things.

I loved Christopher Nolan's *Batman* trilogy, and I've loved, loved, LOVED the Marvel Cinematic offerings so far (with the exception of *Thor: The Dark World*). But I've no interest in *Superman vs. Batman*, I haven't watched a single episode of *Arrow*, and I have no desire to watch the upcoming *Constantine, Gotham,* or *Flash*. I find my interest is waning on the Marvel side of things, as well. I dropped *Agents of SHIELD* after three episodes, have no plans to watch *Peggy Carter*, and I'm sorry, but the Netflix *Defenders* ain't my *Defenders*. I'll probably see *Avengers 2*, just to catch Robert Downey Jr's last hurrah as Tony Stark, but even my excitement for that has waned.

Sooner or later, this superhero bubble is going to burst, because all such bubbles pop eventually, and things run in cycles, and this has all happened before. When it does, a lot of people in film-making are suddenly going to be scrambling to find work elsewhere.

I guess the bright side is that it shouldn't impact comic book sales, because the mythical droves of movie-goers who have never read a comic book and march off to their local comic shop after seeing *Iron Man* and buy up all the *Iron Man* comics are just that—a myth. Oh sure, there have been some, but not enough to boost the entire industry. You also need to wonder, how long before those new readers get burned out by all the gimmicks and crossovers and other things we long-time readers take for granted, but for new readers represent yet one more reason not to bother?

If it sounds like I'm just venting random thoughts, that's because I am. There's stuff going on, behind the scenes. Stuff I don't want to think about. Stuff that might happen today. So I'm just babbling, trying to find some perspective.

Here's some perspective.

If you're a writer, it doesn't matter if your girlfriend just broke up with you or your boyfriend just ran off with someone else. It doesn't matter if your dog just died or the bank just repossessed your car.

That novel you were working on? It's still there, waiting for you.

And also your cat. Your cat is still waiting there, too.

But cats are fickle creatures who will eat your face two days after you are left paralyzed on the kitchen floor by a stroke.

Better to trust in the novel.

It's there. Waiting. Go to it.

People die eventually, but novels—once a novel or a story is out in the world, they're out there forever.

J.F. GONZALEZ R.I.P.

I am heartbroken to confirm what you have probably already seen on social media this morning—my long-time collaborator and one of my best friends, J. F. Gonzalez, passed away earlier this morning after complications from an illness. What follows will be a bit of a balancing act—trying to serve his fans and readers and answer any questions they may have about the status of his future works, while also trying to serve our friends and peers, and also protect his family's privacy. As a result, it will be very long.

J. F. (Jesus) Gonzalez was born in 1964. He was a lifelong fan of horror and weird fiction. His life is one that would make many horror fiction and heavy metal fans envious. As a young man, he hung out on the Sunset Strip in Los Angeles, watching first-hand as many then unknown heavy metal bands (Guns n Roses, Motley Crue, Poison, etc.) soon rose to prominence. He also hung out with the Splatterpunks and other up-and-coming horror writers of that era, again watching first-hand as John Skipp and Craig Spector, David J. Schow, R.C. Matheson, Brian Hodge, and many others rose to prominence. His very first book signing (when he was still just a newbie starting out) was with Richard Laymon and Bentley Little. He had seen and done more in our industry before writing his first novel than many will do in their entire careers.

His first professional foray in the industry was in the early Nineties, as the editor (along with Buddy Martinez) of the horror magazine *Iniquities* (which lasted three issues). It was followed in 1994 with the horror magazine *Phantasm* (which lasted four issues) once again co-edited with Martinez.

From there, Jesus moved on to writing short stories and novels. With Mark Williams, he wrote *Clickers*, a loving tribute to Guy N. Smith's *Crabs* series, as well as other "munch-out" novels such as James Herbert's *Rats* series, all viewed through the lens of H.P. Lovecraft's mythos. In time, *Clickers* became a bona fide, genuine cult classic, earning him a devoted readership.

Clickers spawned three sequels—*Clickers II: The Next Wave*, *Clickers III: Dagon Rising*, and *Clickers vs. Zombies*, all co-written with me. Jesus had asked me to collaborate with him on the first sequel because Mark Williams had passed away and he knew I was a fan of the original novel. We soon found out that we worked very well together, with both of us able to end in the middle of a sentence and pick up where the other person left off without thinking about it. Our styles meshed. Our imaginations meshed. And our love of the genre meshed. I've been lucky enough to collaborate with a number of our peers over the years, and enjoyed every one of those efforts, but with Jesus, it was often like I was writing with myself. He used to echo the same thing.

In addition to the *Clickers* series, we'd recently just finished writing *Libra Nigrum Scientia Secreta* together (which is the last thing he completed before his death—he got sick while we were working on it).

We also had plans for two more *Clickers* books (*High Plains Clickers* and *Southern Fried Clickers*) and a reworking of a novel we were originally supposed to ghost-write for the William W. Johnstone estate, *Day of Terror* (which you can read about in my book *Apocrypha*).

It is *Southern Fried Clickers* that summons one of my happiest memories of Jesus. And I have hundreds of happy memories regarding him, but this one is one of my absolute favorites. We were on a long drive and were bullshitting back and forth, and somehow, we got on the idea for *Southern Fried Clickers*, which would take place in Mississippi and Louisiana. We were brainstorming plot points and scenes and lines of dialogue, and Jesus came up with the idea of the Clickers attacking a Klu Klux Klan rally, and somebody hollering, "That's the biggest damn crawdad I ever done seen!" This caused us both to double over with laughter, because it was ludicrous, and we were exhausted, and punch-drunk, and his southern accent was atrocious. We were laughing so hard that we had to pull over to the side of the road because neither of us could drive. And for nearly twenty-minutes we sat there, laughing. Every time one of us stopped, the other would repeat the line, and we'd start giggling again. By the end, our stomachs hurt and both our faces were streaked with tears.

Jesus's biggest contribution to the genre was undoubtedly his novel *Survivor* (which was born out of an earlier novella called *Maternal Instinct*). Unflinching and brutal and possessing a sharp emotional core, it is often cited along with Jack Ketchum's *The Girl Next Door*, as one of the best extreme horror novels of all time. And it is. But that was a double-edged sword for Jesus. He much preferred to write pulp and supernatural horror, but *Survivor* exploded in popularity, and many readers assumed he was primarily an extreme horror writer instead. He got a chance to address this for himself in *Sixty-Five Stirrup Iron Road*, a novel we co-wrote with Edward Lee, Jack Ketchum, Bryan Smith, Wrath James White, Nate Southard, Shane McKenzie, and Ryan Harding. If you've read the novel, do you remember the chapter where meta-Nate and meta-Jesus are talking to the characters about extreme horror? Trust me, that wasn't fiction. That was Jesus.

Other books included *Primitive, The Corporation, They, Fetish, The Beloved, Restore from Backup* (with Mike Oliveri), *Secrets, Old Ghost and Other Revenants, When the Darkness Falls, Shapeshifter, Bully, The Killings* and *Hero* (both with Wrath James White), *Back From the Dead, Do Unto Others, It Drinks Blood, That's All Folks, Sins of the Father, Conversion, Screaming to Get Out*, and many more.

Jesus was a dear and trusted friend to most of our generation of writers—those of us who started out in the late-Nineties and rose to success in the 00s. You'd be hard-pressed to find anyone who disliked him (other than the trolls, nuts, and crazies who seem to dislike everybody). Every year, he gladly pitched in with Comix Connection's annual Creator Cookout to raise donations for the Central Pennsylvania Food Bank. He was also a big supporter of the Scares That Care charity. He was generous and kind, but he also had zero tolerance for fools or assholes. As I've written about in *Trigger Warnings*, he was an instrumental and core member of the Dorchester War, and that situation would have had a very different outcome without him on our side. More recently, he'd been settling into and enjoying the teacher-veteran-elder statesman role that so many of us find ourselves also settling into, and was genuinely enjoying advising and helping newer creators such as Shane McKenzie, Lesley Conner, and Mike Lombardo.

Most importantly, he was a husband and a father and a brother and a son. Those of us who know him know that he absolutely doted on his wife and daughter, and never made a decision—personally or professionally—without first considering how it would impact them.

Jesus died early this morning, from internal bleeding, following a quick but tenacious fight with cancer. His family were with him and got to say their goodbyes, for which we can all be grateful. Many of you have been wishing him well online this past month. Last week, those messages were passed along to him when myself, Robert Swartwood, and Mike Lombardo visited him in the hospital. Rest assured, he knew that people cared.

In a few weeks, when things have settled down, I'll help his family go through his literary estate. He communicated to me before his hospitalization that he had several half-finished novels and stories under contract, and that I should take care of those. If you are one of the publishers to which he had one of those contracts, please feel free to contact me. If you are one of his lifetime subscribers, you can do the same. Thank you in advance for your patience, and understand that it will be several weeks before we begin to delve into what needs finished and who is owed what, and what remains unpublished, and thus, it will be several weeks before I respond.

He also communicated his desire for me to spearhead a fundraising anthology for his family. Quote: "I've contributed to enough of those over the years. Fuckers better contribute to mine." It will be an invite-only project, mostly among his friends and peers from the early days until now, and I will reach out to those individuals in a few weeks, as well.

For his fans and readers, I can assure you there are more works to be published, but again, I don't yet know the full extent of it. I will update you at a later date.

I know that everyone— friends, fans, peers, readers—want to help. Right now, the BEST way you can help is to purchase one of his books or encourage others to do so. Because Jesus was so judicious in deciding who he worked with (Deadite Press, etc.), you can be certain that the proceeds from those sales will indeed go toward his family.

In closing, I'd ask that you please respect his family's

privacy. You've lost your favorite author, but they've lost a father and a husband and a son.

I fucking miss you already, brother. I made it through this whole thing without breaking down, but I am now, and it's only 2:30 in the afternoon and that bottle of bourbon is looking good. I think I might drink it. Or I might go to that seedy bar you, me, Coop, and Bob went to that one time (the one with the car on the roof and all the bikers inside). I think I might go there and get in a fight just so I can hit something.

And I hear you now, reminding me about responsibility, so I won't do either of those things. Instead, I suppose I should write, but I feel like I've lost my right arm, Jesus, and I can't fucking fathom writing anything after this. Not for a while.

Not for a long while.

I fucking wish we'd become tugboat captains or forest rangers when we had the chance, but I also know we wouldn't have been happy with that, either. Yes, this job sucked, and we both said it to each other all the time, but if not for this job, I would have never met you, and my life would be a whole lot fucking emptier and incomplete as a result. You were right. This tour was cursed, but I also know that it was a blast taking that road with you.

Anyway, you rest easy, old friend, and when you reach R'lyeh, tug on Cthulhu's tentacles and tell him it's from me, and that I'll be along at some point, and that he might as well hand over the keys now. And I promise you I'll keep my promise.

A POEM OR LYRICS OR SOMETHING THAT I WROTE WHILE DRINKING LAST NIGHT

Hello bourbon, my old friend
I've come to drink you up again
Outside's a world I want to throttle
All that's saving it from me is this bottle
And once again, you'll keep me from going to jail
It never fails
Soothed by the sound... of bourbon.

(with apologies to Simon and Garfunkel)

POST-MORTEM ON A MUSE

J. F. Gonzalez, one of my best friends, a frequent collaborator, and a man who was like a brother to me, died this week. Haven't been able to write a word all week long, other than a remembrance and a few words for a *Fangoria* retrospective of his work.

So, apologies in advance if this Blog entry feels rusty. It is rusty. But after a week of not writing, after a week of putting on a brave face for my little boy, and being a rock for everyone else to dash their grief against, and losing myself in bourbon and Pink Floyd's *The Endless River* when everyone else has gone home or gone to bed, it's time to start flexing those writing muscles, shake off the rust, and start writing again.

Yesterday, I spent the afternoon and evening taking inventory of J. F.'s papers and files. This involved meticulously going through filing cabinets and hard drives, collating different drafts of published manuscripts, finding unpublished and unfinished manuscripts, his notes on those uncompleted projects, contracts, correspondence, and everything else that constituted his writing life.

It's a dauntingly intimate thing to go through someone

else's computer in such a manner, and even though I know it's what he wanted and requested of me, and even though I know it's necessary in order to facilitate and advise his family as far as his literary estate, I still felt like an intruder.

It also made me wonder what happens to our muses after we die. I am, in fact, a believer in the mystical muse, as evidenced by my meta-stories "Musings" and "Portrait of the Magus as a Writer (Interpolating Magic Realism)". In the latter, a single muse inspires a group of young horror writers who gather regularly in an online chat room. After they've moved on to various levels of success in their careers, it is revealed that the most successful among them—and consequently, the one who feels the loneliest—trapped the muse in that chat room (which the other authors thought long deleted).

Going through another author's work—not their back catalog but their actual work—their notes and drafts and thoughts that they scribbled down on a cocktail napkin at the bedside at two in the morning—it puts you in direct contact with their muse.

And then you find yourself mourning both.

It's five o'clock. I've been up for an hour. It's time to make coffee and attempt to write.

A REMEMBRANCE OF J. F. GONZALEZ
(FOR "FANGORIA")

Jesus's family used to call him Chuy (pronounced Chewie). He'd get annoyed if anyone outside his family called him by that nickname, so of course, I started calling him that all the time. One day, Jesus and I were on the phone, and my youngest son overheard me call him Chuy, and asked me if Uncle Jesus was my Chewbacca. I thought about it a minute, and agreed that he probably was. Chewbacca was loyal, intelligent, gentle but fierce when the situation required it, did not suffer fools, fought for what he thought was right, and called Han Solo on his bullshit when Han needed it. That was Jesus.

Jesus and I were fans of each other's work before we ever met in person. When we did meet, we became fast friends, and eventually collaborators. We wrote four published novels together, plus a screenplay, and bunch of other stuff. Collaborating with him—one of us could end in the middle of a sentence and the other could pick up where we'd left off. Our voices meshed, our styles meshed, and our appreciation of the genre meshed. I haven't been able to write a word since he passed. I feel like I've lost my right arm, and I'm typing one-handed.

He was so knowledgeable about our genre's literary history—he could discuss everything from Melmoth the Wanderer to obscure H. P. Lovecraft poems to Karl Edward Wagner to Stephen King. And he lived in the center of a great deal of that history over the last thirty years. As a young man, he got to hang out with the Splatterpunks in their heyday. He was there through the rise of authors like Richard Laymon and Jack Ketchum. He was there at the beginnings of the Internet, which changed everything from how horror fiction was published to how horror fiction fans communicated. And he was there through the fall of Dorchester Publishing. He was in the center of all these amazing things, like some sort of horror version of Six Degrees of Kevin Bacon.

He loved horror fiction in all its forms—quiet, extreme, supernatural, splatter, pulp—and more importantly, he was able to write it in each of those forms. Undoubtedly his biggest contribution to the genre was *Survivor*. Unflinching and brutal and possessing a sharp emotional core, it is often cited along with Jack Ketchum's *The Girl Next Door*, as one of the best extreme horror novels of all time. And it is. It definitely is. He could have made a career writing in that same style over and over again, but he was never content to do that. He could write quiet horror on par with Charles Grant or Ramsey Campbell, and then turn around and deliver a cosmic tale in the style of Thomas Ligotti or Laird Barron, and then follow that up with a splatterfest that would make Edward Lee weak in the knees. He was so versatile, and when you read through his backlist—*Clickers, Fetish, Primitive, Bully*, and so many others—it really is quite amazing how fluid his style and voice could be. This has been a huge loss for his family and friends, but it's also a huge loss for our field. He was definitely one of the most diverse, important voices in modern horror, and his loss will be felt for a long time to come.

EULOGY FOR JESUS'S MEMORIAL SERVICE

For those of you who don't know me, my name is Brian. I'm a friend of the family. I'd like to thank you all for being here tonight. We all know why we're here, of course. We're here for Jesus. We're here for Cathy and Hannah. We're here for each other. And we're here for ourselves.

We've come to say goodbye, but more importantly, we've come to celebrate Jesus and remember him.

Jesus didn't want a funeral. He didn't want clergy. What he wanted was family and friends. And love. So that's what we're going to give him tonight, here at one of his favorite bookstores, The York Emporium. We're going to celebrate and remember.

We're going to keep this very informal. Those of you who would like to do so are invited to come up here to the podium one at a time and share a favorite memory regarding Jesus. Maybe you're a loved one whose life he touched. Maybe you're a friend whom he made laugh. Maybe you're a fan who was moved by his work. If so—if you have a special moment or a funny story—please feel free to tell us about it. I'm sure there will be a few tears. And that's okay. Tears are a part of this, and

Cthulhu knows Jesus and I shared a few throughout the years. But we also shared a lot of laughs, and I have no doubt that there will be a lot of laughs to counterbalance those tears tonight.

When everyone has had a chance to speak, we'll mingle here among ourselves and talk and laugh some more, and share a few toasts. There's a bar set up in the back.

I guess I'll get us started.

Jesus was, quite simply, one of the best friends I've ever had. He could make me laugh. Make me think. Make me proud. He was one of the few people not afraid to call me on my bullshit when I needed it—which was often—but more importantly, he was one of the very few who never judged me when he did so.

I met him back in the late-Nineties, and he's been such a major part of my life for the last sixteen years, that it's hard for me to pick just one favorite memory. That's because they're all favorite memories. Be it something as simple as hanging out in the backyard, having a beer, or as fraught-filled as that time the two of us and Bob Ford drove eleven hours in a blizzard from Columbus, Ohio to here while sick with the flu, each memory is special. Each conversation is treasured.

I could tell you about the time we got each other laughing so hard that we had to park along the side of the road for twenty minutes because we couldn't see to drive.

I could tell you about the summer he became convinced that a friend of ours was secretly a serial killer, and how, by the end of that summer, he'd nearly convinced me, as well.

I could talk about how proud he was of Lesley Conner and Mike Lombardo, two of his protégés, and how his pride in them inspired me.

I could tell you about the week we spent at his parent's house, and how funny it was to watch him squirm when they revealed embarrassing details of his childhood.

I could talk about the night he got so drunk he had a two-hour conversation with Nick Mamatas and Kealan Patrick Burke and admitted to me later that he couldn't understand a thing either of them said to him.

I could talk about the Krispy Kreme fiasco.

I could talk about the time we thought we'd contracted scurvy at a book signing.

But the thing I think of the most when I think of Jesus—the thing I want to talk about tonight—is how much he loved his wife and daughter. David Schow and Brian Hodge were both there the night Jesus met Cathy, and both have said independently of the other, that it was like a lightning bolt hit Jesus. I wasn't there to see that, but I damn sure have seen the aura of that lightning bolt, because it never left him. He carried it with him, always.

No doubt tonight a number of you will stand up and say how kind Jesus was. And how generous and sweet and mild-mannered and friendly he was. And you'll be right to do so. But the memory I want to share is one when he was absolutely none of those things.

This is the story of the night Jesus fucking snapped.

We were signing at a convention back in 2007. We'd been at it for ten hours. Ten hours of signing book after book after book. Ten hours with no lunch break. Ten hours of people asking him when he was going to write another book like *Survivor* and asking me when I was going to write another zombie novel. Ten hours of bullshit.

We were tired and hungry and I needed a drink and we both wanted to get the hell away from everyone for an hour or so. But what Jesus wanted to do more than anything was call Cathy and Hannah. That's it. He just wanted to call home.

So we get done signing and we're making our way toward the elevators, and this young author approaches us. He asks if he can buy us a drink and get some advice on writing. I say yes because I've got five bucks to my name and a glass of bourbon in the hotel bar costs twice that amount. Jesus politely declines, informing the kid that he wants to go call his wife, and that he'll come down and join us later.

But the kid won't take that for an answer, and insists on one drink. Jesus reluctantly agrees. We go to the bar. The kid opens a tab, charging the drinks to his room. We order a round. And he starts asking questions. And more questions. And more. And more.

And I can tell Jesus is getting antsy and he hasn't even touched his drink. All he wants to do is go call Cathy and Hannah.

At some point, Jesus brings up Karl Edward Wagner's "Sticks"—a favorite short story for us both. The kid isn't sure if he's ever read it. Jesus begins describing the plot, and the kid says, "Oh, you mean The Blair Witch Project!"

And Jesus snaps. I mean, he just frigging loses it!

"No, I don't mean the fucking Blair Witch Project. What the hell is wrong with you? How can you be a goddamned horror writer if you've never even read 'Sticks'?"

And he's gesturing and berating this kid and slamming his fist down on the table and just going to town. And I very wisely signal the bartender for another round, and charge them to the kid's tab, and just in time, too, because the kid leaves in a huff, looking like Jesus has just stabbed his puppy.

And then Jesus goes up to his room to call Cathy and Hannah and I sit there and drink both our drinks. Eventually, he comes back down to the bar, and he sits down on the stool beside me, and we're both quiet for a minute.

And Jesus says, "I guess maybe I was out of line. But I warned him. I told him I wanted to call home."

That was Jesus. He loved a lot of things in life. He loved good books and good music and good films. He loved writing and he loved his readers. He loved his friends. He loved his parents and his sister. But he loved Cathy and Hannah more than all of those other things combined. I never told him that was what I admired most about him—his quiet, all-consuming devotion to being both a father and a husband. I should have told him that, but I never did.

Thanks for letting me tell you instead.

TRUE WEALTH

We said goodbye to Jesus on Friday night, during a private memorial service at The York Emporium. It was attended by friend, family, and fellow authors, and a lot of folks traveled a long way to be there.

After the memorial service was over, the attendees gathered at various venues to raise a glass in Jesus's honor, including back at my place. The party broke up around 2:30am, after which authors Thomas Monteleone, Drew Williams, Michael T. Huyck, and our friend Joe Branson slept in my spare beds, floor, and couch.

In the late-Seventies and early-Eighties, I used to pedal my BMX Mongoose bike down to the newsstand every week, where I'd buy comic books and paperbacks. One week, I bought a science-fiction paperback called *Seeds of Change* by Thomas F. Monteleone.

Decades later, as I type this, Thomas F. Monteleone is sleeping in my kid's bed, snoring off what will probably prove to be a terrible hangover.

That's not the first time something like that has happened. I had a party once when I still lived in Baltimore. Among the attendees were Richard Laymon and Edward Lee. I had to step out for a bit. While I was gone, Dick and Lee took it upon themselves to go through my library and sign all of their books for me. Obscenely. Riotously obscenely. I still laugh when I read those inscriptions.

And the fan boy who lives inside of me still marvels over it. He marvels over how he's become friends with the very wordsmiths who shaped his life, and how they scribble obscene things in his books when he's not looking, or crash in his kid's bed, or offer support, kindness, advice, and even a hug or a glass of bourbon when he needs it.

On Friday night, friends gathered to say goodbye to a friend.

There are many times I don't like this job. The hours suck. The pay is sporadic. The job security is unreliable. There is no retirement or 401K or health insurance. Your customers can occasionally be assholes, or even a serial killer. But the job itself —the act of writing—is still a joy. And the friends you make along the way more than make up for it.

I may not be wealthy, but I am rich in friends.

Even if one of them—a certain Michael T. Huyck—utterly destroyed my couch last night due to an unfortunate experiment involving beer, bourbon, and absinthe.

BRIAN KEENE'S RULES FOR A SUCCESSFUL PUBLIC READING

1. Unless you are Joe Lansdale, Neil Gaiman, Carlton Mellick III, Chet Williamson, or Thomas Monteleone, never, never, never, never, ever read something over fifteen minutes in length. No matter how good you are or how good the story is, many in your audience will begin to drift away after fifteen minutes (the exception being for those five authors mentioned above).
2. Stories told from a first-person perspective seem to work best.
3. Unless you are adept at doing different voices, avoid stories without dialogue tags, or stories that are primarily a conversation between two characters.
4. Self-contained stories are much more effective than novel excerpts.
5. Make eye-contact with your audience throughout the story. Keep them engaged.
6. Move, if you are able. Don't just stand behind the podium or microphone. Pace slowly back and forth at the front of the room while reading, or even walk

down the aisles. This will further keep your audience engaged and awake. (This rule may not be applicable for all).
7. Practice first. Read it out loud to yourself. Learn the cadence of your words. Learn their pattern. Read your story like you're reading poetry. Learn where to slow down and where to speed up. Project and enunciate.
8. Make it personal. Introduce the story. This can be as simple as saying something like, "This is a story about unrequited love" or as complex as a two-minute anecdote about how the idea for this story came to you during a blizzard.
9. Always have a drink on hand, and know ahead of time where you can pause and take a sip if you need it.
10. Smile, if appropriate. Unless it's a serious story about serious things and a smile would totally mess up the atmosphere. In which case, grimace or scowl or stare thoughtfully at some point over the audience's heads.

THE SCARIEST PART

For me, the scariest part of my new novel, *The Lost Level*, was the book's central conceit—a character trapped far from home in an increasingly hostile and bizarre environment where everything is trying to kill him.

I'm a country boy, raised by country folks, and I have always taken pride in the fact that I'm pretty much self-sufficient. These days, it's trendy to be so. People call it "prepping" and there are books, television shows, websites, and trade shows dedicated to it. Growing up, we didn't learn such skills because they were trendy, or because my parents and grandparents thought a coronal mass ejection would shut down the power grid and summon the zombie apocalypse or because the New World Order were coming to conquer us. We learned them simply because we needed them. Just as a city kid learns skills which helps them traverse the streets and live in the metropolis, we learned how to field dress a deer or run a trout line across the river (to paraphrase the Hank Williams Jr. song).

As a result, I've always been confident of my ability to adapt to and survive any sort of adverse emergency situation. A few years ago, I fell off a cliff while hiking alone, toppled roughly twenty-five feet into a rain-swollen river, got washed downstream about a mile, escaped drowning and fought my way to shore, and then had to hike three miles out of the woods while bleeding from a gash that ran along the entire underside of my forearm.

In the dark.

This was no problem, nor did I have a problem pulling ticks from the wound and then supergluing the gash shut when I finally reached my home. "I can survive anything," I said.

Which is why the universe decided to teach me a lesson not too long ago.

Until earlier this year, I lived in a remote cabin atop a small mountain along the Susquehanna River. Author friends who have visited there can attest to how far removed from civilization this home was for me. It was absolutely perfect, and I loved it. I chopped my own firewood, grew my own vegetables, and had a grand old time living as my forefathers did, and teaching my six-year old some of those skills, as well.

Then the 2014 Polar Vortex hit, bringing hurricane force winds, below-freezing temperatures, and a metric fuck-ton of snow (that's a valid measurement). In the first twenty-four hours, Central Pennsylvania was turned into a disaster area. Millions lost power—and heat. Roads were impassible. Even the National Guard were having a hard time of it. But not me. I sat on top of my mountain, fire roaring in the wood stove, laptop powered by the emergency generator, and feeling all proud of myself for once again being able to survive anything.

That's when the Polar Vortex swung around for a second strike, dropping a tree on my generator, and two more through my roof. Not to mention the thirty or so more trees it dropped across the one dirt lane that led from my home down to the main road at the bottom of the mountain. The woodstove was unusable, the kitchen was full of snow, and the pipes quickly froze and burst. Within hours, my cabin was reduced to uninhabitable rubble (and just like health insurance and 401Ks, working writers seldom have homeowner's insurance, because that's something else we can't afford). And we were trapped, unable to drive out because, even if we made it through the snow, my vehicle wasn't going to transform into a robot and climb over the fallen trees.

It's one thing to teach your child the same survival skills you learned from your father and grandfather. It's another to make him live in a house that suddenly has no plumbing or electricity or heat. So, when the snow melted, we moved to an apartment in town. He is much happier because he has Cartoon Network again, and *Minecraft*, and doesn't have to eat freeze-dried rations for dinner. And I'm happy because he is happy. And while, despite all its challenges, I vastly prefer living in the country over living in an apartment in town, I do have to admit I'm learning an entire new set of survival skills—like how to muffle the sounds of police sirens shrieking or the neighbors partying at three o'clock in the morning. In the country, I secured my trash cans so bears wouldn't get into them. Here, we do the same to keep out feral cats.

We're surviving.

And that's what Aaron Pace, the main character in *The Lost Level*, is doing, as well. He's been transported to an alien dimension full of dinosaurs and robots and cowboys and lizard people. It's a world where even something as innocuous as the grass can kill you. A world where, instead of him saving the Princess, the Princess repeatedly saves him, because he doesn't yet possess the skills to survive there. He's trapped—a stranger in a strange land—with nothing other than what was in his pockets at the time. And he quickly discovers that no amount of readiness or prepping could suffice for what this strange new world has in store.

For me, the scariest part of writing the novel was putting

myself in Aaron's shoes, and remembering what it's like to have your confidence and self-sufficiency shattered and eroded by helplessness and an all-too-consuming despair.

But you know what? You can survive helplessness and despair, too, as long as you don't give in to fear.

NO-SLAVE LEIA

My apologies in advance for the half-formed nature of these thoughts. This really is one of those mornings where I'm typing this right out of bed and before coffee, but there's lots to do today, including rescuing my car from the shop, working on my new novel *Pressure*, and getting a manuscript into the mail.

My seven-year old and I watched the original *Star Wars* trilogy this weekend. In *Return of the Jedi*, many people have been upset over the years by the objectification of Princess Leia aboard Jabba the Hutt's sail barge (slave outfit and all). It occurred to me, however, that the entire Jabba sequence is actually empowering for women.

Consider the following:

1. The Princess rescues her man (Han Solo), rather than the other way around.

2. She's the only one portrayed as having any "guts". Han is a blind and bumbling oaf (thanks to the carbonite) who has to rely on his luck more than ever before, and does a fair bit of whining. Chewbacca is emotional over his friend's condition and spends his time howling mournfully. Lando is consigned to looking grim and pensive and almost becomes dinner for a

Sarlacc. Luke, while heroic, is also aloof, and ends up making a few errors, despite his new Jedi status. And the droids are the droids. Leia, meanwhile, shows cunning, intelligence, bravery, and ruthlessness—the qualities of the stereotypical "hero".

3. It is Leia who kills Jabba the Hutt, and she does so with the accouterments of her objectification (using her chain to choke him while still wearing her slave outfit).

4. Consider the time when this movie came out. While strides were being made on television (*The Bionic Woman, Wonder Woman,* etc.) you didn't see a lot of this type of thing in film. I hold that *Return of the Jedi*, despite its flaws (Wookies in the original screenplay replaced with Ewoks, etc.) was actually an important milestone in the diversification of science fiction.

TO ALL THINGS, AN ENDING

They keep saying Blogging is dead, and it would certainly seem to be, given how little I've Blogged around here recently, preferring instead to simply let this page (and my other social media accounts) stagnate, just like the rest of my writing output.

Depression and borderline alcoholism are motherfuckers.

But I digress. Here's a new Blog entry for you, written in a spare ten minutes between being a father and drowning in work and struggling with the blues. Those ten minutes could be better spent finishing manuscript reviews, or a novel called The Complex (which is due to the publisher August 1st), or proofing galleys for *Where We Live and Die*, or working on the various drafts of *Hole in the World*, *Return to the Lost Level*, *Invisible Monsters*, and *Suburban Gothic* that have all gone off the rails thanks to life and its incessant hammer blows. Or a movie thing I can't talk about. Or some comic book things I also can't talk about (because even though I keep saying I'm done with comics, people keep offering me money to write them, and it's very hard to say no to money because you never know when it will be offered again).

Instead, I'm spending that ten minutes talking about

another ongoing project, *The Seven: The Labyrinth, Book One*. Specifically, I want to talk about the chapter I'm finishing this morning (which should be posted online later this week). This chapter features Ob, the main villain from *The Rising* series and *Clickers vs. Zombies*.

Despite its success and all that it has brought me, I sometimes complain about *The Rising* series. Don't get me wrong. I'm grateful for and humbled by its continuing popularity. That it is still so popular never ceases to amaze me. Not bad for a series of books that started well over a decade ago.

And yet, I still complain. I do that mostly because those first two books are not reflective of anything I write now. It's the work of a much younger, less-skilled writer, and I often wish daily that I could re-write the first novel with the abilities and perception I have now (sort of like Stephen King did for *The Gunslinger*). But I can't, and that's why they call them First Novels.

That urge to re-write them was particularly strong when we released the Tenth Anniversary Author's Preferred Versions of *The Rising* and *City of the Dead*, but I refrained from doing so, even then. I discussed why at length in the Introductions to those editions, but in a nutshell—even if I don't like the books, and want to improve them, there are thousands and thousands of readers who like them just the way they are, and I need to honor that. But yeah, the books that make up *The Rising* series have never been among my favorites of my own work.

Despite all that, it fucking feels delightful to be writing about Ob again this morning, and writing from his point of view, as the city of Dubai burns below him, and I truly begin to draw the curtain closed on this mythos that you, my readers, have grown to love.

I've talked a bit on my podcast and in previous non-fiction collections about certain fictional characters of mine who may have been imbued with a bit of me: Adam Senft from *Dark*

Hollow and *Ghost Walk*, Timmy Graco from *Ghoul*, and to a lesser extent Jim from *The Rising* series and *Clickers vs. Zombies*, and Larry from *Kill Whitey*.

But it occurs to me this morning, as I finish this chapter, that this time, I might be speaking through Ob.

The End is coming, in more ways than one.

Who better than the Lord of the Siqqusim, to narrate it?

FROM THERE TO HERE AND THEN BACK AGAIN

I said "Hello" (again) to Jeff Burk on Friday, and "Goodbye" (again) to J.F. Gonzalez on Saturday, and while I did these things, a young literary group continued to turn on each other, seemingly devouring their own. I woke up this morning (Sunday) thinking about all those seemingly disparate things and how they all actually relate. And although I've got a lot to write today, and although it's not even seven o'clock yet and already my fingers are swollen up like sausages and my back is already in agony and typing for the rest of the day will leave me a physical wreck by the time evening comes, I figured I'd write about this first.

I first met Jeff Burk when he was in college and I was on a publicity tour for a then-new novel called *The Conqueror Worms*. Back then, he was just a kid—a fan of horror and bizarro fiction. Now, a little over a decade later, he's my boss—the head editor at Deadite Press. He's published many of the authors he enjoyed reading in high school—myself, Edward Lee, J. F. Gonzalez, Jack Ketchum, Wrath James White, Bryan Smith, Geoff Cooper, Ryan Harding, and others. He's also a bizarro novelist. His debut novel, *Shatnerquake*, became one of bizarro fiction's biggest bestsellers, and is still very popular years later.

Jeff was in town from Portland, Oregon on his way to the World Horror Convention in Atlanta, Georgia. Friday afternoon, Dave and I had him join us on our podcast, *The Horror Show*. We talked about Jeff's career path, and as we did so, it occurred to me that while I still, in my head, see Jeff as that young college kid who asked me great questions at a signing, he is not a kid anymore. He is a successful adult who has become a driving force in not one, but two genres. He's not a beginner. He's not a novice. This is a man well into his career, occupying a space and a career juncture that I remember all-too-well, and that seems so long ago now.

After recording the podcast, I hosted a small party for Jeff, as I always do for any author that passes through this way. J. F. "Jesus" Gonzalez used to always attend these gatherings, always happy to meet the young-guns and the kids just starting out, and give them advice, if asked. But J. F. won't be attending anymore of my get-togethers, and that realization hit me Friday night, because this is the first one I've hosted since his memorial service back in November of last year.

For a good part of the evening, I listened to Jeff, Bizarro writer G. Arthur Brown, and filmmaker Mike Lombardo discuss all of the in-fighting currently taking place in the Bizarro genre. When asked, I offered my advice and perspective to these younger creatives. Then I paused, expecting Jesus to chime in, the way he always had, but then I remembered that Jesus wouldn't be doing that anymore. I glanced across the sofa at Geoff Cooper, who was sitting quietly, not offering advice, but I knew he was thinking the same fucking things I was, because we'd both been through it before. And so had Jesus.

This in-fighting that seems to have engulfed the Bizarro genre is normal and unavoidable. It's what happens when your genre experiences success. And with Random House now delving into publishing Bizarro fiction, and with networks like Adult Swim looking to Bizarro fiction for possible adaptations, and with actors, directors and name authors from other genres (such as myself or Chuck Palahniuk or Cory Doctorow) talking about their enjoyment of Bizarro fiction, it's fair to say that Bizarro has achieved success. I remember when the only two Bizarro publishers were Eraserhead Press and Raw Dog. Now you've got Strangehouse and Dynatox and a half dozen others (plus, as I said above, the first delving from New York's mainstream, mass-market publishers). Bizarro started out as this cult, underground thing—fiction with a punk aesthetic. It can still be created from that mindset, and it can still wear the trappings of those clothes, but make no mistake—the genie is out of the bottle. Bizarro will never be the small thing it started out as again. After a decade, Bizarro has bred success.

And success breeds contempt.

This is where your in-fighting stems from. It's from people who don't want it to become mainstream, who resent the fact that it's no longer this cult, underground movement. It's from people who feel left behind. It's from people who are resentful of the people who are resentful. It's from people who fear the in-fighting will halt the genre's success. It's from people who prefer one publisher over another, of who prefer one style of Bizarro over another. It's about jealousy. It's about uncertainty. It's about vision.

But mostly, it's about fear—fear of what comes next. Because for the last decade, you've stuck together. You've been a cabal, a tribe, supporting each other and rallying each other and loving each other. Succeeding together and failing together. And now that sense of unity is fraying at the seams, because some people are succeeding faster than others, and some people have different definitions of success, and some people want different things for themselves and their careers and bizarro itself. And at the same time, many of you are having children and starting families and getting mortgages, and you're making decisions based on those, rather than your tribe.

And all of this is okay. It sucks, yes. It's depressing and disappointing and sad, and maybe even infuriating. But it's also normal. And unavoidable.

This is what happens to literary movements. You are not the first. You will not be the last. And if you ask your older Bizarro —writers like Carlton Mellick and Kevin Donihe and John Edward Lawson and Robert Devereaux—they will tell you that they've seen all this before. I know they have, because they saw it with me. Or ask John Skipp, who has seen it happen multiple times.

That's not to disparage or invalidate anyone's concerns. Some of the current arguments in Bizarro—crooked publishers, for example—are the types of things that should ALWAYS be talked about, and ALWAYS be pointed out, even if the discussion is unpleasant. But you must also be cognizant of where others are coming from, and their perspective, and how their own personal fears, uncertainty, or resentment may be coloring their opinion. Everyone's fear is valid. But not everyone's fear is the same.

Anyway, I sat there in my apartment, listening to these three young bizarros discussing these things, and I thought of how Coop, and Jesus and I (and others) had had similar discussions nearly twenty years before, and when I glanced at Coop, I'm pretty sure he was thinking the same thing I was, but I couldn't ask Jesus if he remembered those days, because Jesus is dead. He was taken from his wife and daughter and friends in the space of a month, and I watched him get whittled down to a ghost of his former self, with a speed and rapidity that was brutally shocking, and the last time I saw him conscious he couldn't even speak and I had to do all the talking, and then suddenly there weren't any more collaborations or discussing art and writing and creating, and how we could grow and support our genre, or who we were mad at, or parties, or anything else because he bled out in a hospital bed at three o'clock in the morning and there wasn't a goddamn thing I could do about it.

Yesterday, a group of us moved his wife and daughter into a new home. At one point, Mike Lombardo, Robert Swartwood, and I found ourselves in Jesus's office, packing up his books and contributor copies and manuscripts, and there was a sense of finality about the whole affair. As we packed, we found treasures and heartaches and memories and laughs. Each of us had been in that office many times. We'd sat on that couch and had many of the same discussions with Jesus that the Bizarro are having now.

But yesterday was the last time any of us would ever be together in that space again.

When I was starting out, the horror genre was a small, cult, underground thing still recovering from the financial crash it had undergone years before. For a while, it became a tribe, and everyone stuck together. Then, that fell apart, and we underwent the same phase that the bizarros are undergoing now. And on the other side of that, things continued, and some of us succeeded, and some of us didn't.

I'll turn fifty in three years. I might make it to then. I might not. But looking back, I don't care anymore about which publisher ripped off whom or which writer said something bad about another writer or who got an award and who didn't.

I just miss my friend.

I'd light this industry on fire tomorrow and burn the entire fucking circus to the ground and piss on each and every one of you if it meant I could get him back again for just one more day.

Perspective...

As always, your mileage may vary.

WHAT COMES WITH AUTUMN

Last Sunday, my oldest son David, Coop, our friend Tomo, and I saw Faith No More in concert at Maryland's Merriweather Post Pavilion. We ended up in the front row just a few feet from the stage. Faith No More is my all-time favorite band. It was wonderful to share the experience of possibly seeing them for the last time with two of my best friends and one of my sons.

It was also an exercise in aging.

The last time I saw Faith No More (in the Nineties) I had marijuana for my friends. This time, I had Advil, which both Coop and I took in advance just so we'd be able to move.

The last time I saw Faith No More, the only thing on my mind (other than enjoying the show) was meeting girls. This time, it was whether or not my fading vision would hold up against the stage lights.

Tomo's concern was whether his bad hip would hold up against standing for so long.

Coop's concern was whether his bad shoulder would hold up against any potential moshing or pogoing.

And David's concern was that he wouldn't meet any girls

because he was stuck babysitting three middle-aged men, all of whom are looking at fifty looming in the headlights.

It turns out that David didn't have to worry. We met the girls for him. And I'd like to give a special hello to Dawn who is wise like an owl, and her girlfriend whose name I can't remember. It was lovely meeting you in the front row. And I'd like to give another shout out to Mike and his wife, who recognized me and came up after the show and said hello, and thus afforded David his first public glimpse of "My Dad is somebody other than my Dad".

The concert itself? It was easily one of the top three best concerts I've ever attended. The opening act was Refused (on a reunion tour of their own), and they were phenomenal. And Faith No More has never sounded better or tighter. They started with an explosion and the energy level didn't drop for the next two hours. They looked like they were having fun, and that feeling was infectious among the crowd. This tour has featured a different set list every night. We got "The Real Thing" for an opener, followed by "Land of Sunshine", "Caffeine", and fifteen more beloved songs both old and new, including "RV", which they haven't played live in the U.S. since 1993. The crowd sang along with them all.

I left the show feeling happy and good and at peace with the autumn I find myself surrounded by.

Other than the concert, I've been taking it easy, as per doctor's orders (and in truth, I took it easy during the concert, as well. Before the encore, my body told me to sit down or it was going to drop me. So I listened to my body and headed for the back of the stadium). Taking it easy is defined as not writing more than six hours per day, and getting in an evening walk, and trying not to stress over the insane amount of things I'm behind on or have failed to finish up as of yet.

Thanks to everyone who asked last week, or sent well-wishes. I still feel terribly guilty about canceling my upcoming appearance at the Lewisburg Literary Festival, and I hope to make it up to you next time it comes around.

IMPORTANT THINGS, AND THINGS LESS IMPORTANT

I am house-sitting for my second ex-wife, which means this is being typed in my former office, the place where I wrote everything from the final draft of *Dark Hollow* to the first chapter of *Entombed*. You can see what it used to look like in Mike Lombardo's short film, *Demonstration of the Dead*, which is free to watch on YouTube. It doesn't look like that anymore. These days it's just an empty concrete bunker, devoid of all books and furniture. But there's still a lot of creative energy inside, as evidenced by how much I've gotten done over the last few days. This office was always my most fertile ground, and after my amicable-but-still-tough divorce, I never quite kept up the production pace I used to have here.

I still feel bad about missing the Lewisburg Literary Festival, but on the plus side, I'm pretty much recovered, and I have to reluctantly agree with the doctor. I think another trip so close to the others would have probably done me in. That's something to keep in mind when I start setting up next year's signings and appearances.

While I was recovering, another immediate family member went into the hospital late last week for similar reasons. That person is recovering now, as well, but it was just another reminder of genetics, and the things we carry with us, and what is important, and what is less important.

And time. Everything these days comes down to time.

You might have heard that author Tom Piccirilli is back in the hospital. Tom is another one of my best friends, and has been for the last twenty years. He's like a big brother to me. He has brain cancer. He beat the cancer once, but this time…

Well, everything these days just comes down to time.

A REMEMBRANCE OF TOM PICCIRILLI
(FOR "LOCUS")

Tom Piccirilli passed away last week, after a long and tenacious battle with brain cancer. He was one of my best friends for nearly twenty years. We always called each other "Big Bro" and "Little Bro" because that's what we were. At his wedding, he introduced me as such to his family members. ("This is Brian. He's our little brother!")

But Tom had lots of other brothers and sisters in our field. His professional family was large, spanning across multiple genres—horror, crime, noir, thrillers, westerns, non-fiction, poetry. He wrote it all, traveling from fiefdom to fiefdom on the whims of his always active muse, and the professionals who inhabited those various fiefdoms—who never seem to agree on anything—all agree that they loved Tom.

I met Tom in the mid-Nineties, when the Internet was still in its infancy, and the horror genre was dead and buried. Although he was only two years older than me, he had already experienced some early success, with the publication of two novels, several novellas, dozens of short stories and poems, and a few editing gigs. We used to both hang out in a chat room with other horror writers. Most of the users were novices, but

Richard Laymon, Ray Garton, and Tom were there, freely dispensing advice and encouragement. Laymon and Garton's advice always had the benefit of years—the sage wisdom of authors who had already seen and done it all, and could look back with clarity. Tom's advice was more immediate. Despite his early success, he was right there in the trenches with us, fighting for sales to the same publications, but always cheering us on and offering guidance from his unique perspective. Sometimes, he let his own work slide in order to help us with ours. He warned us about the many snakes and charlatans who inhabit this field. He watched out for us, just like any big brother would.

But his tutelage went beyond professional. Growing up, I was always jealous of friends whose big brothers had turned them on to music or comics or movies that none of us younger kids had been exposed to yet. Tom provided me my first exposure to the films of Alejandro Jodorowsky and John Woo, the writings of Raymond Chandler and Lucius Shepard, and the fever dream that is *Riki-Oh: The Story of Riki*. For years, we regularly sent each other care packages of comic books and movies and old paperbacks. Every time one of those boxes showed up in the mail, it was like every major holiday and a birthday all rolled into one.

There won't be any more of those packages. But he's left behind an incredible body of work, and a ton of memorable advice on the craft. My favorite was always this: "If your response to being stranded alone on a desert island is to scratch stories in the sand with a stick, then you're a writer."

Tom Piccirilli was a writer's writer. But he was also their brother.

Thanks for everything, big bro. I fucking miss you already. Give Dick Laymon and Jesus and everybody else a hug from me.

I'll be along eventually.

FAMILY MATTERS: AN APPRECIATION OF MARY SANGIOVANNI

Mary SanGiovanni is many different things to many different people. She's a daughter, a sister, a mother, an aunt, a partner, a friend, a teacher, an author, and a beloved and vital member of the NECON family. I am pleased to have been asked to write this appreciation of her for this year's NECON (Northeastern Writer's Conference), on the eve of her being presented with the NECON Legend Award.

A graduate of Seaton Hill, with an MD in Writing Popular Fiction, Mary's novels and short stories have enthralled a generation of horror readers. Her Hollower Trilogy (comprised of the novels *The Hollower, Found You,* and *The Triumvirate*) is often credited as one of the inspirations for the widely-popular Slender Man urban legend. Her other works include *Thrall, Chaos, For Emmy, The Fading Place, A Darkling Plain,* and many more. And while her bibliography and professional writing career now span well over a decade, her efforts on behalf of writers should be noted, as well. She was one of the principle proponents of author's rights during the Dorchester Publishing fiasco, and she also teaches writing at a college in New Jersey. A frequent Guest of Honor at various conventions and literary conferences, Mary has talked about writing everywhere from libraries to inside the Central Intelligence Agency headquarters in Langley, Virginia.

Mary decided in high school that she wanted to write for a living. When she asked for advice on how to do this, the school's guidance counselor unhelpfully told her "go to college". While in college, she asked again for advice on how to become a writer. The career placement office told her "write things and submit them." Beyond these platitudes, none of the educators she encountered seemed to know anything else about how to become a professional writer, let alone a professional writer of horror novels.

During this period, Mary worked at a Brentano's Bookstore in New Jersey, where—given her love of the genre—she was put in charge of the horror section. Taking advantage of this position (and a significant employee discount) Mary caught up on the backlist of favorites like Stephen King and Poppy Z. Brite, and was also introduced to a much wider spectrum of horror, including the works of Thomas Monteleone, F. Paul Wilson, Elizabeth Massie, Jack Ketchum, Rick Hautala, Douglas E. Winter, and many more. She wrote at night, and on weekends, and read in-between, but was still unsure of what the next steps to publication and a career as an author should be. The bookstore job led to her encountering the Garden State Horror Writers Group, and it was at one of their meetings that author John Platt changed her life—advising Mary that another thing a writer needed to do was network and interact with other writers. Platt suggested an upcoming writer's conference known as NECON.

Mary attended that year (2001) and was blown away by the experience. All weekend long, she watched and listened to the authors she'd read and admired, the authors whose books she'd stocked and studied, as they laughed and relaxed and talked. That was the most important part—the talk. Given its small, intimate size, NECON was a place where these authors felt comfortable enough to truly talk shop—to discuss the things that don't get repeated online and aren't detailed in countless 'How to Write' self-help tomes. Although she got some advice from author Owl Goingback that first NECON, Mary didn't do much talking herself. In her own words, she spent the weekend awestruck, watching all of these writers who she had admired for so long just sort of playing and having fun. It reminded her in many ways of a family reunion, and the thought of belonging to that community had an appeal to her.

So she went back the following year. And the year after that. And she's been coming back ever since. In convening years, Mary slowly overcame her shyness. Again, in her own words, she wanted to reach a point where this family welcomed her as one of them. And she definitely has. She was the first writer of her generation to be asked to participate in the Game Show. She's served as Toastmaster. She has participated in the annual NECON Roasts, brandishing an incendiary wit that many didn't know she had. She's also displayed an equally gracious sense of humor when she herself was a Roast victim. To quote Mary one more time, some of the most important moments in her life have taken place at NECON. And now she is about to experience another one of those moments.

It is worth noting that NECON has also provided Mary with an opportunity to pay it forward—to offer the same advice and encouragement to beginning writers attending NECON for the first time that she herself received here as a beginner almost fifteen years ago.

But most importantly to Mary, NECON is another family. As I said at the beginning, in the outside world, Mary is a daughter, sister, mother, aunt, partner, friend, teacher, and author. Here at NECON, she is surrounded by a group of peers to whom she is all of those things, as well—a group of people who love her, and who share in the immense sense of pride and accomplishment she feels this year. I know that I certainly do.

Whether you think of her as a daughter, a sister, a teacher, an author, or a friend, I hope you'll join me in telling her about it this weekend.

A TRIP TO MISKATONIC UNIVERSITY

Last weekend, authors Paul Tremblay, James A. Moore, Charles Rutledge, Mary SanGiovanni, Nick Kaufmann, his wife Alexa, and my podcast co-host Dave Thomas, got to visit the John Hay Library at Brown University in Providence—which was the inspiration for H.P. Lovecraft's Miskatonic University.

While we were there, we had the pleasure of viewing many of H.P. Lovecraft's original manuscripts, letters, and commonplace books (notebooks in which a writer records ideas or fragments of stories). Among these gems were Lovecraft's original, handwritten notes for "At the Mountains of Madness (including a sketch he'd made of the monsters from the novella) as well as the handwritten first draft of the novella, a letter to a friend in which he has just learned about Robert E. Howard's suicide and offers his feelings on the tragedy, and the typed draft of "The Call of Cthulhu" (with handwritten corrections scribbled in the margins by Lovecraft himself).We even got to see a mosquito that Lovecraft had squished in a piece of paper, along with a bit of his blood. A particular treat for me personally was the handwritten first draft of "At the Mountains of Madness" and a typed second draft of "The Colour Out of Space"—which are my two favorite works by Lovecraft.

We also got to preview some items from an upcoming public exhibit the library will be hosting later this year. It includes fan letters and artwork a then fourteen-year old Robert Bloch sent to Lovecraft. It was such a treat to view these historic artifacts. The items we previewed are amazing, and I strongly urge you all to see the exhibit when it opens.

My very special thanks to Christopher Geissler, the Librarian for American and British Literary and Popular Culture Collections, for hosting us. He set this entire visit up for us, and was so gracious and helpful and welcoming. Although the public can view scans of the H.P Lovecraft collection online, it's rare that anyone other than scholars and academics get to see these historical items and artifacts in person. We appreciate him giving us the experience, and allowing us to share it with you.

DEAR ROSE: AN OPEN LETTER TO A FAN I MET THIS WEEKEND

Dear Rose,

I met a lot of awesome readers and fans at this past weekend's Second Annual Scares That Care Weekend, a charity horror convention which took place in Williamsburg, Virginia. (And yes, there will be a third one next year).

There was Tom, who is my age, and shipping off to Afghanistan soon, leaving behind his loved ones, and doing it without complaint because that's what he promised to do when he enlisted.

There was Syko, whose name I spelled incorrectly when I signed his books. There was the young couple who I met in the bar on Thursday night (whose names I regretfully can't remember) who were nervous and excited and absolutely wonderful, and laughed with delight when I called their family member (also a fan) and wished him a happy birthday.

And the couple who drove down from New Jersey whose names I also can't remember (the guy wore an Opeth shirt).

And these folks were just the tip of the iceberg. So many great and wonderful people stopped by during the weekend, and I appreciate them all.

But it is you, Rose, who stayed in my head during the six-hour drive home last night, and who has remained in my thoughts ever since. I don't know your last name, and I don't know if you're on social media, and I don't know how else to reach you, so I'm resorting to this. I apologize in advance for using this method, but I'm pretty sure I'll keep your identity secret despite this public letter.

When you came up to my table, I saw the nervousness in your stance and your body language, and heard it in your voice. When you told me you suffered from agoraphobia, I was absolutely blown away. I can only imagine what attending a convention is like for you, especially inside the dealer or celebrity rooms, where masses of people are pressed together like cattle in chutes, and the cacophony of raised voices seems to batter at you from all sides.

Except that, as I told you, I don't have to imagine it, because I get pretty anxious in such situations myself. I'm able to flip my "ON" switch—to transform into the public Brian Keene, rather than my real self, and cope with it long enough for everyone to have a good time, but yeah... when it's all over, I need to go somewhere quiet and sit by myself and be alone and not talk for a long while.

The fact that you braved all that, and came out to support the charity—a charity that is near and dear to my heart—means the world to me. You have my absolute respect and admiration, and I would really be delighted to send you some more signed books. Email me so we can make that happen. And to weed out the pinheads who will say they are you just to get books, tell me the location of that quiet spot I pointed out to you—because that's our secret, known only to us (and maybe also to author Kelli Owen and my podcast co-host Dave "Meteornotes" Thomas).

Seriously, Rose. You rock. You touched me, and your grace and determination are something I won't forget (and that's saying something, because my memory ain't what it used to be. I've apparently met author Armand Rosamilia seven times, and each time has been the first).

Thank you for braving it all to support the charity. The world needs more people like you.

DUST TO DUST

A reminder that next weekend, I'll be speaking and signing books at the 2015 Albatwitch Festival in Columbia, PA. The current schedule has me speaking at three in the afternoon, but I have to leave the festival at 1:30pm to officiate a wedding. Therefore, I'll be speaking at 12 noon. Also, I'll be signing until then just below the intersection of 3rd & Locust Street.

Yes, you read that correctly. I can legally officiate weddings now. So I've got that going for me if this writing thing ever falls through.

Some friends and I took an early birthday expedition to Centralia this past weekend. If you're not familiar with the name, it's a ghost town in Pennsylvania, the site of a massive, sprawling underground mine fire that's been burning for decades. The ruins are the inspiration for a number of horror stories, movies, and videogames, including the very popular *Silent Hill*. It will also feature in the final Levi Stoltzfus novel,

Bad Ground, which I intend to start early next year, after I finish the penultimate novel in his saga, *Invisible Monsters*).

This was my fourth trip to Centralia in five years, and what's remarkable is how quickly the place is changing. Trails I hiked on previous trips have vanished completely. Ruins that were there on earlier visits are gone, reclaimed by the wild. The place very much feels like it's winding down. Ashes to ashes, dust to dust—which is perhaps an apt sentiment for a town that was killed by a mine fire and choked in coal dust and burning ash. In a decade, I strongly suspect all traces of it will be gone.

Here are some examples:

I took a photo of this wall in 2013.

This is how it looks now.

This photo of author Michael T. Huyck Jr. inspecting some Cthulhu graffiti was taken in 2010.

Here is what that same graffiti looks like now. Other visitors and explorers have made their contribution. The graffiti has been added to, morphed, faded, and added to again. It's also interesting to note how the road around it has changed, as well.

But while the wall and the graffiti are still present, there are other things in Centralia that have been completely reclaimed by the wild or swallowed up by the ground, and exist now only in pictures.

This picture of Michael T. Huyck and Geoff Cooper standing on this hillside cliff was taken back in 2010. You can see smoke from the mine fire drifting out of the ground around them.

That entire hillside is now gone. The entire landscape has changed. All that exists there now is a sinkhole, which swallowed up that hillside like it was a bowl of pudding. And the fire has moved on from that location, as well. Indeed, the topography had changed so much, that on this visit, I had to use GPS and a compass just to make sure I was in the same location.

I was there. The hill wasn't.

This picture of me posing amidst a highway full of penis graffiti (which has delighted my friends) was taken back in 2013.

Now, two years later, all of those penises are gone, and exist only in photographs.

In the past year, three of my best friends have died. Two of them were age fifty. Another was a few years younger than me. I turn forty-eight this week.

Soon, Centralia will turn to dust, existing only in photographs. And sooner or later, so will I—existing only in this picture of me and one-hundred graffiti penises that no longer exist, spray-painted on an abandoned highway that no longer exists in a town that no longer exists.

Dust to dust, indeed.

NOW LEAVING THE COMPLEX

Long-time readers will remember that I used to live in a remote cabin atop a mountain along the banks of the Susquehanna River. That living situation changed during the winter of 2013 - 2014 when several severe snowstorms, brought on by the Polar Vortex, rendered the property (and many surrounding properties) uninhabitable. As you may remember, I posted a video of the aftermath online. You may also remember the essay I wrote about it for author Nicholas Kauffman's website.

Living in a devastated remote cabin and roughing it is one thing when you're by yourself. It's another when you've got a young child living with you. And being a prepper (a trendy word for what we country folk just call "being prepared") is all fine and dandy until a falling tree smashes your generator into scrap metal.

In early 2014, my youngest son and I moved into town. Specifically, we moved into an apartment complex. The time spent living there inspired my new novel, *The Complex*. I think *The Complex* is one of the best things I've written in years. The folks who've read it in manuscript format seem to agree. One of them called it "a vicious, violent, conscienceless bastard of a novel—the kind you used to write all the time." And he's right. It is all those things and more—a desperate, harrowing, bleak novel written during a desperate, harrowing, bleak time in my life.

Suffice to say, I've hated living here in the Complex. I'm a country boy, and in the country is where I belong.

Which is why I was elated last week to find a place available back on the river, now that the recovery in the area is finished. And when I say this place is on the river, I mean on the river. The Susquehanna River is thirty-two steps from the front door. There are five bald eagles nesting in a tree in the front yard. There's a vast expanse of woods out behind the house. There's a boat dock, a room for my office, and a room for the podcast studio. To find out how this move will impact the podcast for the rest of the year, tune in to this Thursday's episode (when we will also be remembering T.M. Wright and interviewing Robert Ford).

In the meantime, please pre-order a copy of the hardcover edition of *The Complex*. Remember, you only have until Tuesday to do so. After that, pre-orders end and the books ship —just in time for Christmas. I think you'll enjoy it. And when you read it, know that you're reading a chapter of my life. A chapter that I can now, thankfully, close the book on.

And for those who just can't economically justify a signed, limited edition hardcover, there will be paperback and digital copies of *The Complex*, but not until Spring of 2016—and trust me, you don't want to wait until then because all your friends are going to be talking about it when they get their copies of the hardcover later this month.

THE SAMHAIN BLACKOUT: WHAT WAS SAID AND WHY IT'S IMPORTANT

My apologies in advance for any typos. I started writing this at three-thirty in the morning. It is now six in the morning. This is the first thing I've written in a week, other than a few Tweets and Facebook posts from my phone, and I'm doing so surrounded by unpacked boxes, and using a shipping crate as a desk for my laptop.

Also, I can't find the coffee pot, and suspect it may not have made the move.

So you're going to suffer with me, fuckers.

Don D'Auria is inarguably the top living editor in the horror genre. In his thirty-plus year career, he was responsible for resuscitating mass-market horror from its mid-Nineties grave; getting Richard Laymon back into print in the United States; helping start the careers of then young authors such as myself, J.F. Gonzalez, Mary Sangiovanni, Tim Lebbon, Bryan Smith, and Sephera Giron; and making sure the work of such veterans as Ed Gorman, Ramsey Campbell, and Hugh B. Cave saw new audiences. He's worked with everyone from Bentley Little and Jack Ketchum to new authors like Jonathan Janz and

Adam Cesare. When Dorchester and its Leisure Books imprint imploded (as recounted in my book *Trigger Warnings*), Don found work at Samhain Publishing.

This past Monday, Samhain's public relations department requested that their authors write testimonials about Don D'Auria and post them to social media via the hashtag #Samhain10.

On Tuesday morning—not even twenty-four hours later—they unceremoniously fired Don. To say this came as a shock to him is an understatement. To say that the authors who were asked to write testimonials felt blindsided and used is an even bigger understatement.

On Tuesday afternoon, my phone began dinging incessantly as people began to text me. There were roughly two dozen such texts, all a variation of the same theme—"Did you hear about Don? What the hell is going on?" As stated previously, I am in the midst of moving from an apartment complex back to the country. When these texts started, I was on the back of a U-Haul truck, struggling to lift a bookshelf by myself, and had no access to the internet other than my phone.

I called one of the authors back—Jonathan Janz (who has since stated publicly on his Blog that he contacted me, so I'm not "outing" him here). I asked Jonathan if Don was okay, and I asked him if the authors were okay, and what I could do for both Don and the Samhain authors.

Since I'm transitioning between homes, I went to my ex-wife's house, where I have a spare computer and internet access, and I spent some time talking to other Samhain authors, all of whom were absolutely furious. Some stated they were done with the company, and vowed that they would not work with Samhain Publishing again.

Later Tuesday afternoon, Samhain's owner, Christina Brashear, perhaps seeing the uproar from her authors, released the following public statement, reprinted here in its entirety under Fair Use:

Samhain Horror Changes

As many of you know, Don D'Auria has departed Samhain Publishing, and we wish him great success in his career. His departure was one of several difficult choices we've made recently regarding overhead and editorial support, as we adjust to the evolving marketplace.

While we remain dedicated to making a success of our Horror line and to supporting our Horror authors, due to the slow build of a paying audience we must work more diligently to engage readers. A social media presence is an absolute must because marketing has become about a conversation, and not just about blasting people with ads. Throughout our other lines, Samhain's editorial staff is not only well-versed in curating content and helping it shine through their polishing efforts, but they are social-media savvy and understand how to promote their authors' works. We look forward to bringing this kind of support to our Horror line as well.

In addition to preparing existing contracted books for publication and reviewing submissions, we have the following efforts underway:

Samhain will once again be sponsoring the HWA / Stoker Awards as we have for these past four years.

We have begun planning for the perennially successful HorrorHound Cincy.

We have submitted numerous works for the annual Bram Stoker awards, and look forward with great excitement to those results.

We will be submitting works for the Shirley Jackson awards within the next two weeks.

Our promotional efforts are changing as well. You spoke, we listened and then confirmed your suggestions and ideas through our own testing. Over the past six to twelve months we've been monitoring the advertisements we've bought and have come to the conclusion that banner ads simply aren't selling books. As we pull back from traditional advertising, however, we've begun focusing our marketing dollars on the channels that have proven to work. We've already seen improvement.

In addition, we've begun developing a second Horror newsletter where the authors can contribute and engage, more so than the standard new releases e-blast which is announcement only. Content equates to discoverability. Discovery leads to engagement. Engagement brings about conversions—which for authors, means book sales.

We're proud of our many horror authors and look forward to continuing to bring great stories to readers, as we've done for the past 6 years since launching the line. All authors with existing contracted books will be reassigned to new editors, based on where you are in the publishing process. Look to receive an email on this subject later this week.

In closing, we're very sad to have to see Don move on, but we're dedicated to Samhain Horror and to making it a success. As always, we welcome your feedback, suggestions, ideas and comments, and we sincerely appreciate your work and the stories that you have to share.

Christina Brashear | Samhain Publishing

If Brashear's intent with this communique was to calm authors, her announcement had quite the opposite effect. The Too Long; Didn't Read version—Don was fired because he's not on Twitter or Facebook.

This is an absolute insult not only to writers and editors, but to horror fans, as well. To imply that the job of an editor is nothing more than a social media marketer is not simply tone deaf—it displays the staggering incompetence of a publisher who knows nothing about how the products it sells to consumers are actually made. An editor's job is to read manuscripts, acquire them for publication, help smooth and polish the finished novel, and work with their stable of authors on follow-up books. Their job does not involve Tweeting or Facebooking. That's the job of marketing departments, sales departments, public relations departments (which Samhain has), and the authors themselves. Don's firing sets a dangerous precedent for our industry—at a time when editors are already stretched thin and overworked, do they now have to fear losing their jobs if they are unable to wear yet another hat; a hat that is ill-fitting at best? You don't ask a telemarketer to do a soldier's job. You don't ask a fireman to do a schoolteacher's job. And you don't ask an editor to do a marketer's job. It's as simple as that.

I've known or worked with many remarkable editors in my twenty-plus years in this business. Let me name four of them to illustrate a point—Ellen Datlow, Melissa Ann Singer, Paul Goblirsch, and Larry Roberts. Ellen and Melissa are active on social media. Paul and Larry are not. All four of them are capable, professional editors that any author would be lucky to work with. But take a look at Ellen and Melissa's social media accounts. They're not spending all day selling and marketing books. Do you know why? BECAUSE THAT'S NOT THEIR JOB.

On Tuesday evening, after talking with Samhain authors who wanted to support Don and make their anger with the publisher known, but without costing themselves or their stablemates sales, I suggested online that instead of using the #Samhain10 hashtag, a #SamhainBlackout tag should be used instead. I suggested that since Samhain considered social media branding more important than competent editors, I would unFollow them on Twitter, unLike them on Facebook, and unsubscribe to their email newsletters. That's all I suggested. At no point did I suggest boycotting them financially or boycotting their authors. Indeed, I stated I was against such action.

It was my hope, and the hope of some other Samhain authors who will remain nameless, that the social media blackout would attract attention, and start a public conversation about the publisher's treatment of Don, and their stated methods of marketing books (which I'll get to later in this essay, and which many of their authors find just as infuriating as their treatment of Don).

Later Tuesday evening, we recorded a new episode of my podcast, *The Horror Show with Brian Keene*, in which we covered all of the events up to that point. We also got an exclusive, direct quote from Don himself. That episode will air tonight at seven, and also features a remembrance of author T.M. Wright, reviews of *Crimson Peak* and *Ash vs. Evil Dead*, and a fascinating interview with author Robert Ford, who comes from a twenty-five-year marketing and public relations background, and shares his thoughts on the Samhain debacle, as well.

Tuesday night into Wednesday morning, a small group of trolls with an agenda that basically amounts to "Brian Keene is an asshole because he was mean to us one time when we were being idiots on a message board" hijacked the conversation, implying that I had "called for a boycott", and that "dozens of my fanboys were already boycotting" and that "I was doing this for attention". After reading through Tweets, Facebook posts, and comments on message boards, it became apparent that it was these particular individuals who implied a boycott was taking place. And as for the "dozens of fanboys"? It was one—Kyle Lybeck, who, as an editor for Thunderstorm Books and a promising young writer, hardly qualifies as a fanboy. Further, Kyle specifically stated that his decision to not purchase books from Samhain had

NOTHING to do with me or the suggested social media blackout.

Unfortunately, in hijacking the conversation, these individuals, in my opinion and the opinion of several other Samhain authors I've spoken with, showed a disgusting amount of disrespect to Don, and to the authors they supposedly profess to care about. But by yesterday evening, when it became clear to most people with more than two brain cells that nobody was calling for a boycott, and the only people running around shouting it were a small group of pinheads, the conversation got back on track.

So let's focus on that. I've already discussed above how Samhain's firing of Don because of his perceived lack of "social media savvy" sets a dangerous precedent. But what of their other statement—that Don is somehow responsible for weak sales of their horror line?

It could be argued that, as editor, Don is responsible for acquiring books that will sell. But here's the thing—he was doing exactly that. The lackluster sales had nothing to do with the quality of Samhain's authors or Don's selections. They had everything to do with how Samhain markets and sells books. Here are some free suggestions to anyone at Samhain who might be reading this:

1. Tweets and Facebook posts announcing new books are nice, but your authors should already be doing that (at least the ones who understand how this business works in 2015). You should also consider that constant-reader Fred Fiddlestick might not see your Tweet or Facebook post. In fact, if you have five hundred followers, only about fifty to one hundred of them are going to see your social media posting. But you know what they will see? Advertisements.
2. I must assume your company has a media buyer, or

contracts out to a freelance media buyer. Run print ads in *Rue Morgue, Fangoria, Entertainment Weekly, Bleeding Cool, The Fortean Times,* and *Cemetery Dance.* Buy banner ads on high-traffic websites like *Dread Central, The Outhousers, IGN, The Mary Sue,* and *The Gingernuts of Horror.* Buy radio advertising on *Coast to Coast, Ground Zero,* or *Project iRadio* (disclaimer: *The Horror Show with Brian Keene* is part of the Project iRadio network). You spent money to advertise your romance novels on an electronic billboard in Times Square. Spend the same amount and do the same for your horror line.

3. A presence at the Horrorhound Cincinnati convention is a great idea. But why stay confined to that one regional convention? I understand you're based in Cincinnati, but your readers—and more importantly your POTENTIAL readers—are spread out across the country. They're not going to come find you. You have to go to them. That means attending conventions like SDCC, NYCC, WHC, Scares That Care, Walker Stalker, and all the other big cons (second disclaimer: I am affiliated with the Scares That Care charity and sit on the board for their convention). If it's not cost effective for the company to have a presence at these conventions, then at the very least send your authors.

4. You state that in an effort to reach more readers, you're going to sponsor the Bram Stoker Awards and submit works for the Shirley Jackson Awards. This is silly. I'm not bashing on either award. Both serve their place. I have two Stoker Awards myself, and some of my oldest friends oversee the Shirley Jackson Awards. Both are fine institutions. But the vast majority of readers DO NOT GIVE A

FUCKING SHIT about these awards. These are primarily industry awards, primarily paid attention to by those of us in the industry. If you want to reach other writers, this is a great way to do that. If you want to reach readers—they're not at these awards ceremonies. Fred Fiddlestick works five days a week at the foundry. On weekends, he likes to read a horror novel. He's not taking vacation to go attend the Bram Stoker Awards banquet. He's taking it at the beach with his family, where he'll read yet another horror novel.

5. You need to work on your bookstore presence. Don D'Auria cultivated a line of books and a stable of authors for you that rivaled what he built for Dorchester and Leisure. Until the end, Dorchester's sales were solid. Yours are not. Dorchester's books had a presence in bookstores. Yours do not. Yes, this is the digital age, and people can download books to their Kindle and Nook, but there are also a vast number of readers who prefer to shop at physical bookstores. I know. I talk to them every single day. You want sales? Work out a deal with the chain buyers and get your books on the shelves.

Now, as I said, those are five free suggestions. Any more, and I have to charge you a consulting fee.

There's one more thing I'd like to address. Stop and consider the authors impacted by this decision for a moment. J.G. Faherty, for example. I've been at this for twenty years. I think J.G. has been at it for almost as long. Landing at Samhain was a BIG deal for him, and (in my opinion) a long overdue profile boost. As he said yesterday, *"I'd like to do a blackout, but as one of their authors I feel it necessary to stay connected in order to get all possible info as this mess unfolds. I am 100% behind Don—*

he's the only reason I worked with them in the first place—but I don't want to miss anything important."

Or consider another writer, Glenn Rolfe, also with Samhain. Glenn shared his concerns about a social media blackout with me yesterday. In regards to unfollowing Samhain on social media, he wrote, *"If that's where they plan on focusing selling our titles, then that's notifications that our followers will no longer receive. I get the hard push back against the company. They are way out of line with this decision, but it is a business decision for better or worse. My fear with this #SHBlackout stuff is that it is going to be misunderstood by people and become a complete boycott. I know that's not your intention, but people perceive things differently. And then perception becomes reality. That's my concern. I have already seen people put up the "I'm no longer purchasing from Samhain" posts. You have one of the biggest voices in our world. It's easy for people to read it the wrong way and go off the deep end."*

Now, as stated above, the vast majority of the boycott talk was started by a tiny group of individuals with their own personal agenda. But putting that aside, Glenn brings up a great point and a valid concern. Yes, ignoring Samhain on social media does potentially mean that readers won't be aware of an author's books—but I would put it to Glenn that an author shouldn't be relying on their publisher to sell books anyway. Yes, ideally, that's how it works, but publishers produce multiple books each month, and especially at the bigger massmarket houses, only a few select titles get any sort of promotion at all. The rest are dumped on consumers and bookstores and have to sink or swim on their own. It's always been that way and —just like the equally antiquated returns system of distribution—I don't see it changing. That's why it is so vitally important that you do two things with your career (and this is the same advice I gave Jonathan Janz last summer):

1. You have to be your own promoter. There's just no way around it these days. And that doesn't mean spamming people

and social media and message boards with ads for your latest book or Blog entry. Yes, when you have something new, of course you should announce it. But more importantly, you just need to stay engaged with your readers—be they five or five hundred or five thousand or fifty thousand. Say thank you when they say something nice about your book. Say thank you and I hope you enjoy the next one more when they tell you they didn't like your book. (Block them if they're an abusive idiot, of course). Maybe share a bit about your creative process. Tell them your Top Ten favorite horror movies. Stay engaged. Let them know you're a real person, and not a house name like William W. Johnstone or V.C. Andrews. Don't rely on your publisher to do it for you, because you will always, always, always end up disappointed. As one young lady said on Twitter yesterday, she buys a lot of books from Baen and Tor, but she doesn't follow them on social media. She follows the authors. I'm betting she does that because the authors are real people, rather than corporations.

2. Diversify. Never put all your eggs in one basket. Never sell all your books to just one publisher. Never sign an exclusivity contract (unless you're working in comics, in which case, sign the hell out of that exclusivity contract because you'll get things like health care and retirement with it). If you have a novel coming out from Samhain publishing, great. Sell another novel to another publisher. Approach a small press about doing limited editions of your backlist. Diversify your publishers and you'll diversify your income. But more importantly, you'll have a safety net for when bad things happen. One of the biggest mistakes I ever made in my career was staying with only two publishers (one mass market and one small press) for a period of years early in my career—because when the financial crisis hit, and both those publishers went down, I was suddenly broke.

Bad things happen. I absolutely love working with Deadite

Press, and yes, I do a lot of books with them. But I also do a lot of books with Thunderstorm, and Apex, and Cemetery Dance (and next year Macmillan). Why? Because as awesome as Deadite are, they could go down tomorrow. So could Thunderstorm or Apex or Cemetery Dance. Macmillan could get bought out tomorrow and decide they aren't going to publish my horror-industrial espionage-monster-thriller novel. The only constant in publishing is change, Glenn. You have to be ready for it to happen at a moment's notice, and have your safety net in place.

But yes, Glenn, your concerns are valid, and I'm sorry for responding here rather than on Facebook, but this is the first thing I've written in a week, and I've still got a lot of unpacking to do, and I'd like to sleep at some point, and I'm betting your concerns are shared by others, so I thought this was the best way to address it. In short, I hear you, and I feel you, so let me say it one more time for anyone who may have misunderstood:

In response to Samhain Publishing's firing of Don D'Auria and their stated intent to focus instead on building their social media brand, I have unfollowed them on Twitter, un-Liked them on Facebook, and unsubscribed to their email newsletters. Let there be no doubt, I stand with Don D'Auria, and I stand with the concept that publishing houses need editors—not ad reps acting as editors.

This is not a call to boycott their authors or stop buying their books. I am merely saying that since social media is apparently more important to them than competent editors, I will not engage with them on social media. I don't follow the publisher. I do follow their authors (and I buy those author's books, of course).

You're all adults. You can decide what you want to do. And it's all good, whatever you decide. We can still be friends.

But yeah, if somebody tells you I'm instilling a boycott or inciting my fanboys (which is an offensive term by the way) to boycott, send them the link to this Blog and invite them to kiss my ass. Because for twenty years, that ass has busted itself for the betterment of authors and this genre. And I'll continue to do so because that's what the writers who came before us did for us. And one day soon, when it's your turn, I hope you all will do the same.

We're all in this together—except for the nitwits.

MUSINGS OF A MIDDLE-AGED WHITE GUY
(INTRODUCTION TO "THE DAUGHTERS OF INANNA")

As a kid—growing up in the late Seventies and early Eighties in a small, rural Pennsylvania town dominated by a paper mill and surrounded by forests, fields, and isolation—I assumed that all kids pretty much had the same sort of life I did. I assumed they were all white, had white parents (including a father who busted his ass seven days a week at the paper mill and a mother who stayed at home), listened to country music or rock, were Methodist or maybe Lutheran, took a family vacation every year, and existed in a comfortable blue-collar middle class household.

Sure, I saw diversity on television. *Sesame Street* had Black and Latino and Asian kids, but the set of *Sesame Street* looked nothing like what was outside my window. To me, it was as unrealistic as an angry green guy living in a trash can or Bert continuing to put up with Ernie's bullshit instead of stabbing him to death one night. And yes, I saw diversity in comic books. Diverse characters like Ms. Marvel, Red Guardian, Falcon, She-Hulk, and Luke Cage were there every week when I rode my bike down to the newsstand for a new batch of twenty-five cent

Marvel Comics, but again—the world of the Marvel Universe looked nothing like my world. All of the comic books took place in New York City, and Captain America never seemed to visit rural Pennsylvania.

It never occurred to me that somewhere, there was a black kid my age watching *Mister Rogers* or reading an issue of *Justice League of America* and saying, "This white person's world looks nothing like my world."

Let me tell you what my world looked like. I didn't meet my first, live, in-the-flesh African American until 1983—which is not so long ago, kids. His family moved to our small town when we were sophomores in high school. To the best of my knowledge, they never experienced any sort of blatant racism—no crosses burning in their yard or epitaphs hurled at school—but they were outsiders all the same. They were curiosities. Something new had moved into our world, and none of us knew quite what to expect, or quite how to react to it. I was no different. I befriended the kid (Mike) but my conversations with him were primarily me asking variations of "So, you're black? What's *that* like?"

I graduated high school at seventeen. One week later, I was off to boot camp in San Diego. That was my first time truly seeing the world around me for what it really was—and seeing the people who inhabit that world for who they truly are. Boot camp was a mixing pot—Asian, Latino, White, Black—you name it, we were there, all occupying a small barracks no bigger than a two car garage, and learning to live with each other. And learning about each other. I quickly made friends with a guy from Compton and a guy from El Paso, and I soon learned that they were as curious about my world as I was theirs. Their conversations with me were primarily them asking variations of "So, you're white? What's *that* like?"

For four years, I traveled the world, and saw five of the seven continents. More importantly, I experienced different cultures and different people and different religions and different ways of living. I learned about poverty and wealth, and fairness and privilege. I learned that not every mother stayed at home—and some of the ones who did had no choice in the matter. I learned that not everyone was Methodist or even Lutheran. And I learned that my world—that world I'd grown up in—was just one small part of a much bigger, diverse place, and all of the people who inhabited that world had their own stories. And while all of us, as human beings, had things in common, those commonalities were shaped and informed by our different, unique experiences.

Everyone knows what it is to love, or to lose, or to hope, or fear. These are commonalities. But does a straight person know what it is to be gay? Does a white person know what it is to be black? Does a Muslim know what it is to be Jewish? Sure, maybe in an academic sense. But in a human sense, not so much. What we know is what we are exposed to. What we know is what's outside our window.

And in the entertainment we consume.

I am neither a Social Justice Warrior nor a Sad Puppy (if you don't know what those are, then you haven't been on the Internet in the past year, and for that, I fucking envy you). In truth, I find both groups equally annoying. In my opinion, both groups engage in the same false Left-Right/Conservative-Progressive dogmatic bullshit that has brought real and meaningful discourse in this country to a grinding halt.

What I am, however, is pro-diversity. Diversity should be championed by all, regardless of your political affiliation or any other identifier you and the social media tribe of your choice choose to use. Diversity informs us. It educates us. It helps us understand the other inhabitants of this planet—the people who don't live outside our window, but are just as much a part of things as we are—a little better.

And in the entertainment we consume, diversity offers

unique perspectives and fresh takes on tired, worn-out old tropes. As a white kid, I read about and identified with a white kid named Peter Parker who was secretly the superhero known as Spider-Man. Today, black and Latino kids can read about and identify with a black and Latino kid named Miles Morales who is secretly the new Spider-Man. The stories remain the same. There are the same struggles, the same villains, the same archetypes. But they are informed by a new perspective, a new view of the world, and that makes for invigorating and exciting reading.

In our own field, horror fiction has been way ahead of some of our related genres in terms of diversity—both in the stories told and in the authors writing those stories. "But Brian," someone is shouting from the back, "if we've reached the point of true diversity in horror, then why are you editing and publishing an anthology with only women writers? Why no men? That doesn't seem fair." Well, I'm doing it because I'm Brian Keene, and I'm lucky enough to have some power and a voice in this field, and I enjoy using that power and voice to support things I believe in. In this case, I believe in these four authors. Once you read them, I think you will, too.

Chesya Burke and Livia Llewellyn are undoubtedly familiar to some of you. Both have been writing and publishing in the genre for about a decade now, to considerable critical acclaim. Rachel Deering is known for her work in comics, where she's earned several award nominations. Amber Fallon is a newcomer, with a handful of small press appearances. All of them deserve a wider audience. And you, dear reader, deserve to be reading them.

I mentioned earlier that in the entertainment we consume, diversity offers unique perspectives and fresh takes on tired, worn-out old tropes. That's what happens in the four novellas you are about to read. All four authors have delivered uncomfortable, harrowing, gut-wrenching works of horror fiction, and each one has been informed by their own individual experiences and their own unique voice. Each one is the world outside their particular window.

That's what good fiction is made of.

Take a look, if you dare...

BRAVE NEW WORLD

Last Sunday, sixty-six-year-old Jose Sandoval Opazo, an electrician employed by Carnival Cruise Lines, was crushed to death by an elevator aboard the cruise ship Carnival Ecstasy. Witnesses described "a sheet of blood" and a "waterfall of blood" running out of the elevator. We know this because those same witnesses took extensive cell phone videos of the accident.

Think about that for a moment. When witnessing this gruesome accident, the first reaction of these tourists was not staring in horrified shock, or screaming, or hiding their eyes, or safeguarding their children, or running away, or trying to help. Their reaction was to whip out their cell phones and film videos of the quote, "waterfall of blood" that was pouring from the walls and the crack between the elevator doors.

Two nights ago, as New Year's Eve celebrants did their thing around the world, a young man collapsed unconscious onto a London street. *The Daily Mail* reports in their write-up that he "drew concern from his friends". In a photograph accompanying the article, we see a young man sprawled unconscious in the street, arms and legs akimbo. His friend sits on the curb next to him. The newspaper claims this is one of the concerned friends, but the picture shows this second youth staring at his cell phone and typing a text message, rather than calling emergency services or assisting his companion.

Our culture is bombarded every day by atrocity after endless atrocity. ISIS has a multi-million-dollar media production team churning out videos of them slaughtering people. Methods shown in these Hollywood-quality videos include beheadings, stonings, firing squads, throwing them off buildings, having them drawn and quartered, dragging them behind cars. The footage of this barbarity is as slickly produced as Disney's new *Star Wars* movie, and is churned out to the Internet for people to watch on their cell phones.

But it doesn't stop there. Traffic accidents, riots, robberies, fights, shootings, sexual assaults—in case after case after case we learn that a bystander, instead of displaying any normal human reaction (fight or flight) is simply whipping out their cell phone and capturing the moment—a moment which is then viewed a million times on other people's cell phones. Perhaps this is a subconscious way of removing themselves from the danger or separating themselves from the trauma. Perhaps the phone acts as another witness, a safe space from which to view what's happening around them.

Or maybe we're just becoming desensitized as a culture.

Yes, pictures of atrocities always existed before, but they weren't readily available, nor did the average person seek them out. The Allies hid the photographic evidence of the Nazi's worst crimes to protect public sensibilities (and also because they feared their people would rightfully demand greater, swifter action). Rape porn (not the pretend fantasy stuff but actual rape committed on film) has existed since film was invented, but it's not something you found by typing a simple Google search. Yes, Romans could watch people beat the shit out of each other until one of the opponents was dead in the

Colosseum, but now we can watch the same thing filmed live from any city street on any Saturday night. And don't get me started on the parents I see out with their children—all staring at their cell phones instead of talking to their kids.

What purpose, then, does horror fiction serve in this brave...nay, *desensitized*... new world? From the time of cave paintings and *The Epic of Gilgamesh*, up through *Melmoth the Wanderer* and *The Lottery* to *The Stand* and *IT*, horror fiction has served as a safe space—a way for artists to reflect and examine humanity's fears. A way to examine what's out there in the darkness, and to examine the darkness lurking inside all of us, as well.

If that darkness is now dispelled by the light from a touch screen, or worse, if that darkness is simply the heart and core of an entire generation of human beings, what happens next?

In his review of my new novel *The Complex*, S.J. Bagley of *Thinking Horror* said, "Keene has managed to fully integrate the emotional core of the work (particularly the sense of disbelonging, willful exclusion, parental anxiety, and deep sense of close proximity social anxiety) with the plot happenings... This may be the best novel I've read from him." Filmmaker Mike Lombardo said, "The narrative perspective is removed—cold, like a camera lens, which makes it that much more powerful."

Now, I don't claim that *The Complex* was an examination of this new, seemingly desensitized culture we're living in. Or, at the very least, it's not what I consciously set out to write about. And yet, it's there in the subtext, unknown to me, the artist, but readily apparent to readers. It's also there in Paul Tremblay's *A Head Full of Ghosts* and Bryan Smith's *Slowly We Rot*, inarguably two of the most popular horror novels of the past year.

I predict we'll see more of this in horror fiction for 2016. I can see the future...

...when I look up from my phone.

NORMAL PEOPLE'S JOBS…AND SLEEP PATTERNS

I often wonder about normal people, and by normal, I mean anyone who was smart and didn't end up working as an entertainer or an artist for a living. I wonder about their jobs. More specifically, I wonder about how their jobs relate to their sleep patterns.

Do nurses wake up at four in the morning thinking about a patient's medication? Do schoolteachers wake up at four in the morning thinking about their lesson plans?[1] Do mechanics wake up at four in the morning with a solution to fix muffler bearings?[2] (Disclaimer: I don't know if muffler bearings are a real thing or not, but my knowledge of automotive repair is slim enough that it could fit into Nickolaus Pacione's bibliography of professional sales).

I ask because I woke up at 4am, bolting upright in bed fast enough that I severely startled my cat, Mad Max, who had been sleeping on my chest. He glared at me and then settled back down next to the fireplace, but I barely noticed, because the reason I'd woken so suddenly was that I'd figured out what to do with the Clickers.

Clickers for new readers, was a horror novel by J.F. Gonzalez and Mark Williams. It was intended to be a homage to the "munch-out" horror novels of the Seventies and Eighties—things like James Herbert's *Rats* series and Guy N. Smith's *Crabs* series. Especially the latter.

Clickers earned quite a dedicated fan-base for its time, and had the distinction of being one of horror's first true ebooks. Unfortunately, Mark Williams passed away before it ever saw publication. When the book became popular and fans asked J.F. for another, he asked me if I'd like to take Mark's place on the sequel. We wrote *Clickers II* together. That was followed by *Clickers III* and *Clickers vs. Zombies*. We had plans for at least two more Clickers related projects—a comic-book series called *High Plains Clickers* (which would have been set in the Old West) and a new novel called *Southern Fried Clickers*. Unfortunately, J.F. passed away before we ever got to write those.

I've talked at length on two podcast episodes and a little bit on the forum about my reluctance to do anything more with the Clickers, and how, although J. F.'s loved ones would like to see it continue, and the fans would like to see it continue, I didn't feel right doing one on my own.

Which is why I bolted upright at four this morning, with an idea in my head of how it could be done—of how I could deliver one last Clickers blow-out to the fans, and do it in a way that would be respectful of J. F. and Mark, and also in a way that would involve all of their friends and peers.

More on that later. Right now, I need coffee…

---

1. Author Sarah Pinborough has assured me that when she was a schoolteacher, she often woke up at 4am to solve schoolteacher-related problems.
2. Author Christian Jensen, who also works as an auto mechanic, has assured me that auto mechanics also get up at 4am with solutions to problems. He did not confirm if muffler bearings were a real thing, though.

MEMO FROM THE SICK BED

Yesterday, Paul Legerski and Queensryche's drummer, Scott Rockenfield, hung out all day while I was dying on my sick bed, but Paul was nice enough to send me a picture of the two of them backstage. Scott is holding a battered copy of Dark Hollow. He and Paul are both grinning. The picture is captioned 'Get Well Soon'.

Thanks guys.

I write three hundred and sixty-five days a year. The only time I don't write is when I'm sick. And I haven't been this sick in a very long time. Which might explain why I've got it so bad right now. Fever, nausea, trembling like Michael J. Fox over a fracking site in Oklahoma, and congestion unlike anything I've ever experienced. I swear, at one point, something crawled out of my nose, dripping with slime, and learned to walk on two legs like a human.

Or that may have been a fever dream.

Anyway, instead of writing, I spent the day in bed. And I

spent that time in bed reviewing manuscripts for other authors, reading John M. McIlveen's *Hannahwhere* and Joe R. Lansdale's *Fender Lizards*, and listening to albums (Johnny Cash's *Original Sun Sound*, Metal Church's *Blessing in Disguise*, Motorhead's *No Remorse*, and Bruce Springsteen's promo version of *Born in the USA* that contains "Jersey Girl", "Pink Cadillac", etc.) at a low volume while my cat, Mad Max, spent the day asleep on my feet.

Now, that may not sound like work. Well, maybe the first bit—reviewing manuscripts for other authors—sounds like work, but listening to music and reading? That's not work, right? Wrong. Artists, be they musicians or painters or writers or filmmakers, don't consume entertainment like normal people. Art inspires all of mankind, but what art inspires in other artists is the desire to make more art.

So, reading the latest from John M. McIlveen and Joe R. Lansdale or listening to Johnny Cash and Metal Church on vinyl—that's done on two levels for me. The upper level is that I'm playing the role of a consumer, and consuming that form of entertainment and enjoying it for what it is—a book or an album. But there's an underlying level, that of an artist, who is soaking up inspiration during the experience.

Joe R. Lansdale directly inspired my novel *The Lost Level*, my short story "Lost Canyon of the Dead", and probably a few other things I've written. Johnny Cash (in conjunction with Trent Reznor) directly inspired my short stories "I Am An Exit", "This Is Not An Exit", "Exit Strategies", and "The Man Comes Around". Bruce Springsteen's music directly inspired my short story "Johnstown".

Everything is inspiration. Everything is grist for the muse—even when we don't think it is. Even if we're not aware of it happening. Not all of it sticks. Sometimes a book is just a book, a movie is just a movie, and an album is just an album. But more often than not, for creative types, art inspires other art.

I don't yet know what the art inspired by John M. McIlveen, Joe R. Lansdale, Johnny Cash, Metal Church, Motorhead, and Bruce Springsteen channeled through a 102-degree fever and a constant influx of NyQuil and ginger ale will be, but I'm sure I'll find out down the road.

I passed out for a while. When I woke up a few minutes ago, I went back and re-read what I wrote above. I can't tell if it will make sense to anyone else but me or not. My head is full of green NyQuil clouds, and more things have crawled out of my nose and lungs and are now shuffling across my backyard toward the river, in some sort of bizarre reverse evolutionary funeral march.

There's probably a story idea in that hallucination, as well.

SOME THOUGHTS ON LIVING AND DYING

I was talking privately with some fellow author friends yesterday—Geoff Cooper, Mike Oliveri, Michael T. Huyck, and John Urbancik. These are guys I've known for over twenty years now. Guys who I have representations of tattooed on my back. They are those kind of friends.

They were talking about growing older, and the changes everyone is going through, and the possibility of death. This was all inspired by the fact that another of our friends who is also our age, Jack Haringa, was recovering from open heart surgery.

A few of us (I won't say who) feel as though perhaps death is stalking us, and who knows? Maybe death is. In the last two years I've lost three dear friends. Our industry has lost even more than that. Perhaps death is indeed stalking us, or stalking me, at the very least.

But if so, then death can take a number and get in line, just like everyone else on my trail.

Anyway, this is a slight permeation of what I wrote, during our conversation about death. I've taken out a few personal details, and changed the names of my sons (my oldest is referred to as Grunge and his little brother is referred to as Turtle), and added a few things to clarify, but the rest stays intact. I'm posting it here because I owe you a Blog entry today, and I'd like to do one that's not just a link to other things, and also because I'm worried that my thoughts on suicide (which are voiced in tonight's episode of my podcast) will be misconstrued or misunderstood by some listeners.

"The truth is, boys—I'm ready for it. I'm ready for death. Now, don't get me wrong. I don't want it to happen. I don't want to die. Turtle is too young to be put through that. We all know what Pic went through, losing his father at such a young age. I don't want to put Turtle through that same kind of pain. And truthfully, being his Dad? It's the thing I'm best at and the best thing I've ever done.

But between Pic and Jesus and Jason and everybody else that has passed recently, the fact is—we ain't kids anymore. Yes, anyone can die at any time, but as we get older, the odds change. As someone who has spent his life beating the odds, I'm all too aware that they're getting more and more difficult. I think we're all aware of that, aren't we? John's had heart surgery, Dave's had heart surgery, and now Jack is having heart surgery. We are not kids. We are not angry young men. We are well past that stage of our lives.

With that in mind, I half expect it to happen at any time. When Coop showed up at the studio yesterday to record this week's podcast, my heart was giving me trouble. It gave me trouble throughout the broadcast. And that's with meds, exercise, eating right, etc. Sooner or later, my heart is going to pop. If it doesn't, I'll get cancer or get stabbed by some nut at a book signing or maybe die in a horrible blimp accident over the Rose Bowl on New Year's Day.

So, I've got my shit in order—literary estate, instructions for the rest of Jesus's literary estate, regular will, Turtle's college, etc.

I hope it won't be soon. I'd like to see Turtle graduate and become whatever it is he wants to be. I'd like Grunge to make me a grandpa in a few years, if he's ready to do that. I suppose I'd like to get a Lifetime Achievement Award to go along with my Grandmaster Award.

But if it happens...if I die, I'll be at peace with it, because I've accomplished what I set out to do, and my kids love me, and my ex-wives and ex-girlfriends have all forgiven me my sins. I've had an awesome life, in retrospect. Yeah, there were a lot of dark times, but there were good times, too. It was a life lived to its fullest. I've had a pretty spectacular run. I've had some amazing adventures. I've seen almost all the world. I've laughed and drank far from home. I've had more than my fair share of romantic partners (not as many as Lemmy, maybe, but it's not like I was out to break a record) and have been lucky enough to have loved many and been loved by many. I've cheated death, I've been to jail, I've driven fast into the sunrise, walked slowly into the sunset, walked through forests and deserts and everything in between, and danced naked in a few of them, too. I've held babies and puppies. I've gotten wisdom from both the old and the young. When I was a kid, I wanted to walk on Mars, and I still do, but other than that, there's nothing I truly desired to do that I haven't already done. I wanted to be a writer. I wanted to write things that brought people joy. Here I am, and I did it, and I still do it on occasion.

So, no, I don't want to die. I may be afraid when it happens. But I'm also at peace with it if and when it happens. I'm at peace with the certainty that it will come. I've had a spectacular run.

Anything from here on out is just gravy..."

THE END OF THE BRONZE AGE OF SUPERHERO CINEMA?

I grew up during the Bronze Age Marvel and DC comics—the name given to the era of comic books published in the Seventies and Eighties, much of which has informed the Marvel movies and television series thus far. Many people my age lament the post-Bronze Age comic book product for various reasons. Some cite the fact that the characters have changed too much from their core, while bizarrely offering the illusion of no change. Others argue it is just the opposite of that. Many decry the corporatization of comics, with creation by committee, story lines by synergy, and a greater adherence to intellectual property farming and brand management than natural growth.

For myself, there's just nothing there in modern comic books that interests me. I grew up with Peter Parker. I got bullied when he got bullied, got a job around the time he got a job, got married around the time he got married, etc. I have no interest in reading about a Peter Parker who is perpetually twenty-something and still has all his hair and whose knees and joints never hurt. I would have a great interest in reading about an almost fifty-something Peter Parker who is all of those things, and who is training a young man like Miles Morales to be his replacement.

But I digress.

Yesterday, my seven-year old and I went to see *Star Wars: The Force Awakens* again. This is our third time seeing the film. He has zeroed in on the character of Finn the way I zeroed in on the character of Han Solo when I was his age. The first time I saw *Star Wars* in the theatre, I was eight years old. When we left, I tried to get my father to pretend his pick-up truck was the Millennium Falcon and he and I were Han and Chewbacca. My father, who was never one for imagination, declined. Upon seeing *The Force Awakens* for the first time, my seven-year-old asked me to pretend my Jeep Cherokee was a Tie Fighter and that he and I were Poe and Finn, escaping from Starkiller Base. I did, happily, and we played it the entire way home. He loves *Star Wars* and I love watching him watch and play and experience *Star Wars*.

But I digress again.

On yesterday's outing—our third—we saw the trailer for *Captain America: Civil War*. My son informed me that he doesn't want to see it because the superheroes are busy fighting each other. He had the same reaction to the trailer for Batman vs. Superman. He wants his heroes fighting bad guys, rather than other heroes. And this mindset isn't limited to my child. Soccer dad that I am, I talk to and hear from other kids his age—both boys and girls—during play dates, cub scouts, sports, etc. All of them are echoing variations of this theme. For a multitude of reasons, their interest in the upcoming superhero movies is very low. Their interest in the next *Star Wars* movie is very high.

I'll be curious to see how this plays out over the next five to ten years. Are we going to see the films begin to wane in popularity as a younger generation—the iPad generation—begins to lose interest at the same time older viewers such as myself tune out as the movies begin to mine for material the same story lines we walked away from years back?

WHAT NEIL GAIMAN, BRIAN KEENE, AND YOU NEED TO DO TO BE A WRITER

Today, social media worked itself into an outrage...

Wait, let me start over, because social media works itself into an outrage every goddamned fucking day.

Today, social media worked itself into an outrage and decided it was Neil Gaiman's turn. On Twitter, Neil offered an endorsement of the Clarion Writing Program, with which he has a long history (something that is no different than say, me Tweeting an endorsement of the Scares That Care charity). Neil Tweeted: "clarion.ucsd.edu is where you apply to go to Clarion. If you want to be a writer, you want to go to Clarion, NEED to go to Clarion."

Immediately after this, approximately two hundred and twenty thousand Tumblr warriors and would-be writers poured their outrage onto social media, accusing Neil of everything from classism to being a paid shill. As is standard operating procedure for the internet outrage machine, they did this based on that lone Tweet, disregarding and ignoring the volumes of Blog entries and essays Neil has written about becoming a writer, and advice to such.

The only thing Neil was guilty of was engaging in hyperbole and failing to consider that, as large as his audience is, there are probably more than a few wingnuts in it who will take issue with anything he says or Tweets. As author Nick Mamatas said earlier this evening, "Aspiring writers are always hysterics but any writer handing out advice should know that and avoid expansive claims." Could Neil have worded that Tweet more carefully? Sure, maybe. But he's Neil Gaiman and everybody loves him and he probably genuinely didn't ever consider there would be a blow back like this—because why would there be? Hitting Neil Gaiman is like shooting into a barrel full of puppies.

Now, me on the other hand? I commit more accidental micro-aggressions before breakfast than most people do all fucking day. So let me explain to you what you need to do if you want to be a writer.

You need to write every day.

That's it. That's all.

You need to write every day. You need to find an hour in your day and you need to sit down and you need to write. Writing does not constitute playing Xbox or looking at funny GIFS on the internet or talking about writing with other writers. Writing involves sitting your ass down in a chair and committing words from your head to either paper or screen.

Going to Clarion or any other sort of writing workshop or MFA certainly won't hurt your chances. They will probably help. But not everyone can do that. I never went to Clarion or any other sort of workshop. I never went to college. Hell, I barely graduated high school. Despite that, I've done okay for myself, with over forty books in print in fourteen different countries, and a dozen literary awards, and even a few movies. I bring people joy. I entertain them. And I'm able to feed my children doing so.

I achieved that by sitting in a fucking chair and writing every day.

It doesn't matter what genre you're writing in, or whether your sentences are short or long, or how many followers you have on Twitter, or how many Likes you have on Facebook, or how many times your Tumblr Blog about Spider-Gwen's new costume was shared. It doesn't matter which writing organizations you belong to, or which writer's groups you're a member of online. It doesn't matter where you went to school, or what workshop you attended, or whether you got published via New York or a small press, or indeed, whether you got published at all. None of those things make you a writer. Getting published doesn't make you a writer.

What makes you a writer is sitting in a chair every day and writing.

"Oh, Brian. I can't. I have kids, a job, parents, school, Fallout 4 to play, the new season of Jessica Jones to binge watch..." Bullshit. So do I. So do all of us. You're no different than anybody else. If you want to be a writer, you make the time to write. You get up an hour early, go to bed an hour later, skip your lunch break, dictate it via a voice recorder during your commute, etc.

You find a way. That's what you need to do. That's all you need to do. But you'd be surprised how many would be "writers" can't commit to that. Instead, they'll write about not having time to write.

SOME OBSERVATIONS ON CROWDFUNDING AND SOCIAL MEDIA

As of this morning, the Kickstarter campaign for *The Naughty List*— a short film directed by Paul Campion (*The Devil's Rock*) and based on my story "The Siqqusim Who Stole Christmas"— is sixty-six percent funded. That's sixty-six percent funded in the first twenty-four hours, mind you. We announced it yesterday morning, and promoted it throughout the day via social media.

So, what was the secret to our success? Here are my observations on what worked and what didn't work. None of this is scientific, of course, but after twenty years in this business, I think my record for divining successful self-promotion is pretty solid. I'm sharing this information so that it might be of use to other creatives and artists who are considering launching a Kickstarter campaign.

Twitter worked wonderfully. I have over eleven thousand followers on Twitter. Every time I Tweeted a link to the Kickstarter page yesterday, I saw an immediate and demonstrable bump in pledges from them.

Facebook worked terribly. I have over nine thousand followers on my public Facebook page. Every time I posted a link to the Kickstarter page on Facebook yesterday, approximately thirty-nine people out of those nine thousand followers saw each post. That's because Facebook's algorithms detected the link embedded in the post, and then buried it. Why? Because Facebook wants to charge users advertising fees for more views. The one Facebook post where I didn't include the link, and instead told people to get the info at, quote "Brian Keene dot com", was seen by a much larger percentage of users. This further solidifies what many of my peers have been saying in private—and what Warren Ellis has been saying out loud. Facebook is fine for staying in touch with childhood friends, but as a marketing and promotional tool—it sucks. Unless you want to spend money. And it's going to continue to suck. Facebook is in the very early stages of going the way of MySpace, I imagine.

The forum at Brian Keene dot com worked pretty well. Not nearly as well as Twitter, but if we parse the numbers—the forum has five hundred and forty users, eighty of which were online at some point yesterday. Of those eighty, approximately sixty of them visited the thread for The Naughty List and then clicked through to the Kickstarter page. A perhaps shocking but true fact is that those are much better numbers than the ones from Facebook.

I didn't bother promoting the Kickstarter on Instagram or Tumblr. In the case of the former, most Instagram users are not going to click through. That's not how they use the service. They use the service to look at pictures. And in the case of Tumblr—the vast majority of the users on Tumblr are either too young to participate in a Kickstarter, or would find something problematic and socially wrong with the project itself.

So, there you have it. Make of my raw data what you will.

I STILL WANT TO BELIEVE

As hard as it is to believe, *The X-Files* was not a ratings blockbuster during its first season. I started watching the show with the original airing of the third episode, and as far as I know, I was the only one of my friends doing so. The show took off in ratings and popularity with seasons two and three, but that first season? It felt like it was just mine.

The night I first saw *The X-Files*, I was a young twenty-something father, working a blue-collar job and trying to become a writer, had just gotten divorced and—much to my dismay (and theirs)—had temporarily moved back in with my parents. That living arrangement lasted two months, ending when I'd saved up enough money to start over again. But my love an enjoyment and devotion to *The X-Files* has lasted ever since.

I've always sympathized with Fox Mulder's quest. There are things in my background, things I experienced, things I don't talk about or share with nearly anyone—public or private. Only a very slim few know about them. Suffice to say, I always wanted Mulder to find the truth, because it was a truth I sought, as well. But Mulder and Scully's search for the truth goes beyond alien abduction and government conspiracies. At the core, it's a search for answers—to what happens when we die, is there anything more than this, who's in charge, does the universe have order, or is it just a chaotic joke? Their quest was one that appealed to our human spirit—and that's a quest that never gets old.

Mulder's gotten older. Scully's gotten older. Skinner's gotten older. And I've gotten older. And yeah, that premiere last night was a little bumpy in parts (episodes two and three, which I've been lucky enough to see in advance before they air, are much stronger). But regardless of the bumps, it was good to see those characters again. Good to know that somebody else is still searching, and still asking. Because the truth is still out there, and I still want to believe.

This is a good time to remind you that I made my own contribution to *The X-Files* universe, with a story about Skinner in the anthology, *Trust No One*, available now in paperback, eBook, and audiobook. It's a story that did not come easy, because I wanted it to be perfect. Therefore, it took a long time to write.

Our individual quests for individual truths can take a long time, as well, but they are always worth it, as long as you desire to believe.

THE PARABLE OF FRED AND LUCAS

Fred likes Team A. Team A professes to represent all of the things that Fred believes in.

Lucas likes Team B. Team B professes to represent all of the things that Lucas believe in.

From now until November, Fred and Lucas will show their team spirit, trumpeting their support of Team A and Team B on social media, at work, at dinner, and everywhere else they go. They'll watch their teams compete on television. They might put signs in their front yard, sharing their enthusiasm with their neighbors. They may even wear shirts or hats emblazoned with the names of their favorite team players. They will root for their team, and ultimately support their team with money and the act of voting.

In November, Fred will vote for Team A and Lucas will vote for Team B. But who they'll really be voting for is Team C.

Team C isn't on the ballot. Team C doesn't need to be on the ballot. And no matter what the ideological differences are between Team A and Team B, it is the policies of Team C that ultimately get put into practice. If Team C decides that Fred and Lucas should be punched in the nuts, then Team A and Team B will punch Fred and Lucas in the nuts.

And four years from now, Fred and Lucas will vote for them to do it all over again.

That's voting in America in 2016.

ONE STAR CIVILIZATION

Writers, publishers, and booksellers have a long list of problems with Amazon. My big problem with them has always been a little different. My problem with them is their Customer Review process.

I don't mind a one-star review that is based on the merits of the book. That's a valid thing, whether I agree with the reviewer's position or not. But we've all seen one-star reviews that say things like "I think this e-book costs too much so I'm giving it one-star" or "I didn't read this book, but I find the subject matter offensive, so one-star." This is ludicrous, it is wrong, and it directly impacts the author's wallet. It's the equivalent of a writer showing up at your job in the warehouse and saying to your supervisor, "I know Bob is a forklift driver, but he packed chicken salad for lunch today and I hate chicken salad, so dock ten bucks off his pay next week." Even more baffling to me, is that this process directly impacts Amazon's profit, as well—yet they allow it to continue.

Reviews, be they positive and five star or negative and one star, should inform you about the product in question, be it a book, a movie, a record, etc. And while many Amazon customer reviews do just that, they are invalidated every time Amazon allows some brain-damaged howler monkey to hammer out a review of their own.

For example, known stalker and serial harasser Nickolaus Pacione, having been temporarily banned from Twitter, Facebook, and other social media, took to Amazon's customer review system to Blog about his private life. In a five-star review of a Beanie Baby, he rants about charges of child abuse against him, and makes threats and accusations against the family member who brought those charges against him. How is any of this drivel conducive to helping a customer make an informed decision as to whether or not they wish to purchase this product?

Another example, unfolding right now, is the novel *Only by Blood and Suffering*, written by Robert LaVoy Finicum. For the uninformed, Finicum was one of the militia members who recently seized federal land in Oregon as part of a protest against Eminent Domain laws in our country, and other grievances. Now, I'm not going to get into the man's politics, other than to say I think both his group and other recent protest groups such as Black Lives Matter all raise important points, and it's a shame they can't listen to each other and find common ground, rather than seeing each other as antagonists from the other team.

But I digress.

Robert LaVoy Finicum was killed last night during a stand-off with FBI agents and local law enforcement, allegedly while surrendering with his hands up. When you read the reviews for his novel on Amazon, legitimate reviews based on the merits of the book are lost amidst a flurry of one-star and five-star reviews from people who admit to not having read the book, and are instead basing their reviews on their feelings regarding the stand-off, his death, and their own politics.

And it happens to everyone. The Amazon page for my

friend Chuck Wendig's *Star Wars* novel is filled with bogus reviews by people who admittedly did not read the novel and are protesting the erasure of the old Star Wars novels from continuity. Reviews for books by Presidents Bush, Clinton, Obama, and candidate Trump are filled with political posturing, rather than anything having to do with the content of the books. The Sad Puppies troll the reviews sections of John Scalzi's books. The Social Justice Warriors troll the reviews sections of Larry Correia's books. Doctor Who fans leave reviews based on whether or not they like the actor depicted on the cover.

The bottom line is this. Amazon's Customer Review process is in need of a serious overhaul. It's something that is long overdue. As it stands right now, it's a shopping experience akin to going to a brick and mortar bookstore, and picking a novel off the shelf by an author you're unfamiliar with, and attempting to read the back cover synopsis while a raving, unwashed lunatic stands next to you shouting about the dead fish living in his pocket and how you should pet it.

Now, I don't know about you, but if I'm shopping at a bookstore, and a raving, unwashed lunatic begins shouting at me to pet the dead fish living in his pocket, I'm not going to buy the book. Instead, I'm going to put the book back on the shelf, leave the store without making a purchase, and go home to re-read one of the four thousand books I already own.

And if enough people do that, it's not good for anybody in this industry.

Except for maybe the guy with the fish.

GUNS

I often confuse people who don't really know me, because I'm not Conservative or Progressive, and I get equally annoyed with both camps. When people hear me expounding an idea that leans Leftward, they assume I must be a Democrat. When they hear me expressing an opinion that leans Rightward, they assume I am a Republican.

Take my stance on guns, gun control, and the Second Amendment, for example. I see people online all the time who incorrectly quote my stance on this topic, and it's gotten so out of hand that I feel compelled to clarify my thoughts.

I grew up... well, not poor, but there were a lot of years where what my Dad shot during hunting season helped fill the gap in the groceries so my parents could pay the other bills instead. This was especially true in the years when the union at the paper mill where my father worked was on strike.

So yeah, I learned about hunting at an early age. I shot my first gun when I was twelve. This was done under the watchful eye of my father, with strict supervision and a lot of training beforehand. I've shot all my life. I'm not a hunter. I went hunting when I was younger, mostly because it was a way to spend time with my old man, but I don't enjoy hunting and it's not something I participate in as an adult. I'd much rather just watch a deer or a rabbit, than shoot them. Maybe take their picture if anything. But I do enjoy target shooting, and I'm good at it. Indeed, without bragging, I'm a certified expert marksman. For me, target shooting is as relaxing and enjoyable as any of my other hobbies—reading, fishing, painting, listening to music.

People think, maybe because of the size of my arsenal—which I admit, is probably a little obscene—that I'm some right-wing gun nut or a member of the National Rifle Association. But I'm not. I loathe what the NRA has become, and I quit the organization many years ago. I think the gun lobby industry in general is a blight, and it makes me want to puke every time there's a mass shooting and they immediately turn it into a political football and shout about how Obama is coming to take everybody's guns. I'll be the first one to admit, I'm not crazy about the Obama administration, and there's a lot of things that have happened that I don't agree with. But the man has been in office eight years, and guess what, assholes? He didn't knock on my door and take my guns.

But you know what? I also loathe the jackasses on the Left who do the same fucking thing, and make it all about how we should completely ban guns.

We don't need to ban guns. But we also don't need stupid people owning guns. I think the answer is simple. You need a license to drive, a license to fish, a license to own a dog, and a license to get married. I think you should be required to have a license to own a firearm, as well. And if you're an idiot—if you leave that gun out where a kid can get ahold of it, or you wave it around while drunk, or wear it strapped over your shoulder while shopping at fucking Wal-Mart, then they should take your license away. Permanently. And there are other gun owners, hunters, and target shooting enthusiasts who feel the same way I do. The problem is, we get shouted down by the extremists on both the Right and the Left.

I think we also need to take a look at the already existing gun laws. We need to enforce the ones we're not enforcing, and maybe change some of the others. For example, I own an AR-15. I bought it legally. It's a fun gun to plink at bottles with. But you know what? I don't really need it. It's not a practical gun for deer hunting (if I was a hunter). If they passed a law tomorrow that said, "We're not selling any more AR-15s at Wal-Mart", I'd be okay with that. But I'm not okay with "Let's get rid of all guns." I'm not okay with it because on two separate occasions, a gun has saved my life and the life of my loved ones (once against an animal and once against an intruder).

We also need to take a hard, honest look at our mental health care in this country, but that's an essay for another time.

My point is this. There is common sense, logical middle ground to be found on this country's gun debate. The problem is, the lobbyists on the Right and the Left don't want the rest of us to find it, because then they're out of a job.

SUCCESS CHANGES

Many people in this industry will tell you that I am an asshole. And if you don't know any people in this industry, then Google will tell you the same thing. Now, I like to think that I'm decidedly not an asshole. I don't think my kids think I'm an asshole. I don't think my girlfriend thinks I'm an asshole. I don't think my ex-wives think I'm an asshole (at least not anymore). And I don't think my friends—my real friends—think I'm an asshole, either.

So why do some persist in saying I am? I don't know that it's any one particular reason. I suspect, rather, it involves several factors.

Publishing—and indeed, the entertainment industry as a whole—can be a refuge for bullies. Now, understand that I'm not saying every editor, critic, publisher is a bully. Most of the people in this field are fine individuals. But bullies certainly do exist in our industry.

And I hate bullies.

I was bullied by these two guys from first grade through sixth grade. I mean, just day in and day out. Oh, sometimes I got a reprieve, if they found somebody else to bully instead. But for the most part, I was one of their favorite targets. I can't tell you how many comic books, bubble gum cards, and Star Wars action figures these guys snatched from me in elementary school, or how many black eyes or ripped shirts I came home with. It lasted until I finally decided that I had had enough. The next time they bullied me, it was in the school cafeteria. I hit the first one before he could hit me, and I knocked him flat on his butt. He lay there, astonished, gaping up at me. To be honest, I was pretty stunned myself. So stunned, in fact, that I forgot all about the second bully until he started kicking my ass. I had braces on my teeth at the time, and he punched me so hard in the mouth that my braces got stuck in the flesh of my bottom lip. In pain, and feeling embarrassed, I ran away and left school property. Eventually, a teacher found me, and took me to the nurse, who pried my bottom lip off the braces and then sent me off to the principal's office, where the other two bullies were seated, as well.

While we were waiting to talk to the principal, the second bully started crying, worrying about what his father was going to do when he found out his son had started another fight. I told him if that he gave me his entire comic book collection, I'd tell the principal I started it (this was in the Seventies, and school policies and discipline were very different than they are today—all that mattered to the people in charge was who started the fight). The second bully agreed to my offer. The principal didn't believe a word of it, but no other witnesses were stepping forth, and long story short...those two guys never bothered me again and I amassed the biggest comic book collection in all of sixth grade.

I hate bullies. I've never forgotten how it feels to be bullied, to be the underdog, and that has put me at odds with a certain element within our field—usually misogynistic troglodytes or racist assholes or publishers who think contractual terms are more of a suggestion than a legally binding document. At times, I've been criticized for "bullying bullies." If that's true... well, so be it. I'll wear that hat. I'll wear that hat because somebody fucking has to. Experience has taught me it's the only thing bullies ever respond to.

I think another aspect in regards to why people think I'm an asshole is my success. Truth be told, I've been lucky enough to have an enormous amount of success in our field, starting with my first published novel. I know this, I recognize this, and I am grateful for this. They say that success changes people, and maybe that's so—but I think what changes is how people react to the person who has had the success.

I like that so much I'm going to start a new paragraph and reiterate it. Success doesn't change the person who had the success. It changes how people react to the person who has had success.

Because once you've experienced success, people expect you to help them achieve it, as well. Now, I try to do my best in that regard. I'm not above helping others achieve success. In fact, it's something I believe very strongly in. But there are only so many hours in a day, and I can't help everybody all the time. People get resentful of that. They think you aren't doing everything you can for them. Or they think that because of your success, you must have Stephen King money. Nobody has Stephen King money, except for Stephen King. Or they think you got to where you are by some fluke, because they don't see the twenty years of busting your ass that you put into it. Or, perhaps worst of all, they ask for your advice and you give them your advice and then they ignore it and get pissed off at you when things don't work out for them the way they wanted them to.

And you're the asshole.

I guess the final factor in why people think I'm an asshole is the fact that I can be a little cocky. A little brash. This was probably more so when I was younger. I think I've mellowed with age. And a lot of that perceived arrogance from when I was younger was really just me joking around. I've always suffered from a small dose of social anxiety, especially in large crowds. Being a clown helped ease that a bit.

But I still call it like I see it, and I don't have time to mince words because, again, there are only so many hours in a day. I think some would like me to mince my words a little more? Make them more palatable? But... this industry is full of people blowing smoke up each other's asses. I'd much rather somebody be honest with me. Smoke and empty accolades aren't going to help you succeed. They aren't going to assist you in becoming a better writer or avoiding a bad deal. Only truth does that.

At the end of the day, I'm a father to two boys. One is twenty-five. The other is seven. Those are two very different skill sets, trying to be a father to boys that age. They each require different things from me. My responsibilities to them come before my obligations to anyone else. I do what I can to help people, but I also do what I can to maintain my own peace of mind and personal space and responsibilities to my kids. If there are people who don't understand that or can't respect it, then those are people I don't really want in my life anyway.

Success is knowing that you're a good father and a good friend.

WHAT IT TAKES TO BE A BESTSELLER

Twenty-four hours after it went on sale, the Kindle edition of *All Dark, All the Time: The Complete Short Fiction of Brian Keene, Volume 2* is currently sitting at #9 on Amazon's bestseller list for horror short story collections, right behind the new Peter Straub collection, a Dan Padavona collection, and a bunch of books by Stephen King. How many copies did it have to sell to get there? Forty-four.

These days, forty-four copies in twenty-four hours will land you on the bestseller list.

A name also helps you become a bestseller—and it doesn't even need to be your name. As I mentioned before, if you take a look at that bestseller list, you see collections by myself, Peter Straub, and Dan Padavona. You also see Stephen King's latest collection firmly ensconced at #1. What books are between Steve's latest and myself, Peter, and Dan? At first glance, those other books are also by Stephen King—except that they aren't.

Welcome to another one of Amazon's dirty little secrets—the world of scam artists masquerading as popular authors and utilizing Kindle's self-publishing technology to make a quick—and crooked—buck.

Looking at the bestseller list, you'll see *Awaken* and *Descendants*, two new short story collections ostensibly written by Stephen King. But they aren't. They're written by somebody pretending to be Stephen King. Stephen King has never written books called *Awaken* or *Descendants*. And understand, this isn't a case of an author simply having the same name as him. It's a case of outright fraud. The author bio for *Descendants* is the real Stephen King's bio, which the impostor copied and pasted. That's right, he stole the real Stephen king's bio.

If you go to the listing, directly above the bio, you'll notice that Amazon themselves are apparently aware of this malfeasance, because they've included a note that directs readers "looking for Stephen King the bestselling author of *Doctor Sleep* and *The Shining*" to his author page.

Now, I don't know what we can determine from this, but to the casual shopper, it would appear that they are concerned enough to direct readers to the other Stephen King, but not enough to actually remove the fake Stephen King's books from print, or at least move that disclaimer to the top of his listings, where customers are more apt to see it.

As if that wasn't confusing enough, there's also a second fake Stephen King.

Why does Amazon allow this to continue? Because they're making money off of it. And despite the amount of one-star negative reviews and customer complaints, I don't expect they'll be changing it anytime soon.

So what can you, a reader, do about it? There's only one thing I can think of. Put *All Dark, All the Time: The Complete Short Fiction of Brian Keene, Volume 2* along with Dan's new collection and Peter's new collection, up there in spots #2, 3, and 4 (in any order—I'm not greedy) so that the fake Stephen King is below us in the rankings.

That will show him!

FIVE MINUTES OF FAME, FIVE MINUTES OF FRIENDLINESS

There are different kinds of fans. Most fans, you will never meet and never hear from. Other fans may reach out on social media and tell you they enjoyed or hated something. A smaller subset will follow you with fervor. And there's an even smaller subset that you get to know so well—you find yourself becoming friends with them, or at the very least, familiar acquaintances whom you recognize right away and perhaps exchange holiday cards with. That's how it started with people like Mark 'Dezm' Sylva, Stephen McDornell and Tod Clark. They were in that last subset at one time. Now, I consider all three friends. I trust them enough to let them pre-read everything I write. The same happened with folks like Valerie Botchlet, Paul Synuria, Mark Hickerson, and Deb Kuhn, who moderate the forum. I met them as fans, but over the years we've drank together, shared hotel rooms together, gone through divorces and break-ups together, and genuinely become friends.

Mark and Paula Beauchamp fall into that final subset, as well. I've known them since around the time *The Rising* first came out (so 2003). I've talked with them many times, hung out with them many times, and signed many books for them. I haven't hung out much with their daughter though, until last year.

I'm not going to mention her name or age here, because she's a little girl and I want to protect her privacy, but Mark and Paula brought her to last year's Scares That Care charity horror convention and I got to spend a few minutes being nice to her, and being a clown, and making her laugh, and signed a book for her. And the charity's organizer, Joe Ripple, gave her a *Walking Dead* photo signed by some of the cast. And this little girl has carried those two moments with her throughout the year, telling classmates that she's "friends with Brian Keene and Joe Ripple".

She recently had a birthday. She asked her parents if, instead of presents, she could ask for money for the charity. And as a result, she raised nearly $350 for Scares That Care.

All because of five minutes of kindness from Joe and myself.

The moral of this story for you, the new writers, actors, musicians, artists and other entertainers reading this, is to make those five minutes count for the person on the other side of the signing table. It's not always easy to do that. If you're at a convention, and you're seven hours into signing books and you'd really just like to go up to your hotel room and call home and maybe order some room service and just sit very quietly and not answer any more questions about when you'll write another zombie novel—it's not easy to remain on and affable. But do it anyway, because you'll meet some great people out of it. Make those five minutes of interaction count. And the person you do it for? They'll carry it with them long after those five minutes are over.

WHY AND WHEN I WILL BEGIN BOYCOTTING THE HWA

The HWA (Horror Writers Association) is a non-profit organization founded in 1985, for the purpose of promoting the interests of Horror and Dark fantasy writers, publishers, and other professionals in the field.

In its thirty-plus year history, here are some of the ways it has promoted the interests of Horror and Dark fantasy writers, publishers, and other professionals in the field:

- Allegations of a former President embezzling membership funds.
- Allegations of a former President and Vice-President delaying publication of the newsletter until a story regarding possible malfeasance within their administration was dropped.
- Multiple, multi-year allegations of inaccuracies and inconsistencies in the Bram Stoker Award nominating and voting process.
- The organization's failure to act or protect their members when the editor of an HWA anthology

spent the advance on home repairs rather than paying it to the writers in the anthology.
- Former officers, including multiple Presidents, who used their position in the organization and official organization communications to lobby their own works for the Bram Stoker Award.
- The organization's negligence in allowing known stalker Nickolaus Pacione access to the membership directory, which he then used to obtain the home addresses and phone numbers of a number of members, whom he then threatened and harassed, and the organization's slow response to this despite increasing reports from members that it was occurring.
- Forgetting to hold elections for officers in 2016.
- Numerous elections inconsistent with the organization's bylaws.
- The organization's refusal to respond to the Dorchester Publishing debacle, or to act on behalf of its members who were impacted by said debacle, until public pressure from their members forced them to.
- Ditto their Samhain Publishing response, and their Permuted Press response.
- Asking members to vote twice (and reportedly three times in some cases) in the most recent Bram Stoker Awards voting process. (NOTE: See update below.)
- The public relations disaster in which several prominent HWA members (including the then-President) cyber-bullied the innocent daughter of serial killer Dennis Rader, aka BTK, including body shaming and comments about her mental health, which was then picked up by national press.
- The public relations disaster of the current

President's exclusionary and dismissive essay on what constitutes a professional author, which earned the ire and recriminations of prominent members of the field including Neil Gaiman, John Scalzi, and Chuck Wendig.
- The organization's refusal to let valued and prominent members of the community such as bestselling writer Carlton Mellick III join because he was self-published.
- And most recently (as of today) allowing David A. Riley, an avowed white supremacist and fascist who has previously demonstrated a bias against others based on their race, religion, etc. to participate as a Bram Stoker Award Jury member—an award which will include candidates of various races and religions.

Those are some of the ways the HWA has promoted the interests of Horror and Dark fantasy writers, publishers, and other professionals in the field. These are the tip of the iceberg.

Who is responsible for letting these things happen? The HWA membership, and the fact that new members don't know their genre's—or organization's—history and are therefore doomed to repeat it.

But that excuse stops today. Today, the HWA released the following statement regarding their decision to allow an avowed white supremacist and fascist serve as a Bram Stoker Award Juror. Quote: *"The HWA does not support discrimination of any kind, including discrimination based on political views. Not only is this form of discrimination specifically illegal in a number of U.S. states, HWA's Board of Trustees also does not believe it's in keeping with our principle of supporting and practicing freedom of expression. In specific regard to HWA's Bram Stoker Award juries, the HWA will certainly act if/when a juror's personal views have a provable impact/bias against a writer or his/her works."* End quote.

So, I'm speaking now to all current members of the HWA. If, after today, after learning that the HWA will allow this to continue—if, after today, after learning that the HWA will allow a person who has previously demonstrated a bias against others based on their race, religion, etc. to participate as a Bram Stoker Award Jury member—an award which will include candidates of various races and religions—IF AFTER TODAY, you intend on renewing your membership and paying membership fees when they come due again on January 1, 2017, or if you are paying to attend any of the organization's Stoker Cons or awards banquet events in future years, then you are part of the problem.

Effective immediately, I will no longer work with the HWA or any of its regional chapters in any capacity, official or unofficial.

Effective immediately I will not participate in any HWA-sponsored event, including Stoker Con, Stoker Award banquets, or any future World Horror Conventions in which HWA acts as an official partner or underwriter.

Effective immediately I will refuse any future award I may be given by the organization, including any potential Lifetime Achievement Award. ("What about the two Bram Stoker Awards you already own?" several of you are asking. In truth, I'll keep them, because it is my hope that when I die my sons can flip them and all my other awards on eBay and make some money off of them.)

Effective 1/1/17 (when the new year's memberships become active) I will no longer work with anyone who is a then-Current member of the HWA, including writers, publishers, editors, etc on anything sponsored by, presented by, or affiliated with HWA. I will not give cover blurbs, introductions, or anything else. I will not promote events. If I am asked to be in an HWA-affiliated anthology, I will decline. If I am asked to submit a novel, and the publisher is a then-current HWA member and their line is being endorsed/underwritten/sponsored by HWA, I will decline.

So... if you'd like to work with me on anything in 2017, or you'd like my help with something going forward, I'm very happy to—provided it's not something connected to, affiliated with, or supported/underwritten by the HWA as of January 1, 2017. Consider this an eight-month notice, which I think is more than fair.

I realize that this decision will put me at odds with both dear friends and fellow mutually-respected peers. That's okay. It won't be the first time that has happened. But this is my decision. I am not a Conservative or a Progressive, and I hold the extremists in both camps with contempt. But I am a human being, and a father, and I know what is right and what is wrong. Discrimination of someone based on their race, religion, gender, etc. is wrong.

We endorse things by our participation in them. Think about that for a moment. Let it bounce around inside your head.

We endorse things by our participation in them. This current debacle—and previous debacles—are not things I endorse, and I will not, in good conscience, contribute my name, my money, my talent, my draw, or my platform to them. I'm not asking anyone else to follow suit. But I have championed this genre for over twenty years, and I'd like to think I've done my part in promoting the interests of Horror and Dark fantasy writers, publishers, and other professionals in the field. It is my belief that the HWA has not, and that their actions impact not just their members—but all of us who make up this community. Therefore, I can no longer be involved in any aspect with anything connected to the HWA.

. . .

UPDATE #1: Nearly twenty years of posts like these have taught me one thing—wait a few hours, and invariably, the bits that people are misreading will become clear. This is especially true for Facebook skimmers. So, to clarify a few things.

- It was not implied above that all of these are recent grievances. Indeed, some of these stretch back to the late-Nineties/early 00s. The list is to demonstrate that somewhere along the line, the train came off the tracks and it has remained there, regardless of which administration is in power. I stand by my assertion that it is important to list these, as it demonstrates a pattern. And as Jeff VanderMeer said on my public Facebook page, "I've had nothing to do with HWA for more than 15 years because of the pattern." The pattern is the entire point.
- In some cases (self-publishing for example) the HWA eventually changed its stance. But it is a demonstrable record of being slow to act and respond to things that impact the interests of Horror and Dark fantasy writers, publishers, and other professionals in the field.
- HWA member Patrick Freivald writes "The extra voting this year was due to a technical glitch in the database—a regrettable thing but nothing even kind of seedy, painted as something rather seedy." I agree it wasn't seedy. But there were MANY HWA members who expressed frustration and confusion over how it was communicated and handled. Again, demonstrating a pattern.
- Things that are allegations are reported above as just that.
- Some of these things are old news to those of us who have been around a while. For younger writers and

newcomers, this is their first time hearing about some of it. That's why it's important to have the conversation.

UPDATE #2: I have amended and clarified paragraph 12, which begins "Effective 1/1/17..." after a suggestion from Stephen Dorato in the comments below, because the way it was phrased was causing confusion with some (my fault—I should have communicated more clearly).

UPDATE #3: HWA have just released the following statement. Quote: "In regards to the situation involving David Riley, who announced on his blog that he would be serving on the Anthology jury: We've reached out to Mr. Riley, and both Mr. Riley and the HWA have agreed that it's in the best interest of all for him to step down. Mr. Riley will be replaced on the jury immediately by Nicole Cushing. The HWA thanks Nicole for stepping up, and we would also like to thank everyone who has shared their opinion on this matter." End quote.

My dear friend (and HWA member) John Skipp asked me if I will continue to personally boycott anything affiliated with, sponsored by, or underwritten by the HWA were this outcome to occur. Now that it has, in fact, occurred, my answer is yes. Yes, I will.

I used to be one of those HWA members who sought and battled to change the organization. As former President David Niall Wilson said online today, there used to be a lot of us who sought to do that. We discovered that it was impossible for us to do so.

I believe there are a number of fine next-generation individuals currently inside the HWA who wish to change the organization (some of whom have also sounded off in the comments below), and while I respect and applaud their efforts, that is not something that will happen overnight or next week or next month or next year. There is a systemic pattern of incompetence (as demonstrated in the initial post) that goes back decades. Every time HWA steps forward to fix a scandal, things are forgiven, and everyone returns to normal, and then another scandal occurs. This is damaging to our industry and community. It is my personal belief that the HWA does more harm than good to our field and its practitioners, and my decision to no longer interact with it, endorse it, or lend my name, talent, or platform to anything officially associated with it stands.

I'd be happy to change that stance, but first you'll have to prove me wrong...

As always, this is one person's opinion.

Your mileage may indeed vary.

A LITTLE WARMTH AGAINST THE WINTER

It's been suggested by many scholars throughout the centuries that entertainers and artists have four stages to their career. This is a theory that I believe to be true. It is not lost on me that I'm now entering—or am already into—the third stage of my own career (a realization that some of my peers are coming too regarding their own careers, as well).

During the third stage of his career—when he was living more off his reputation and the past than any new written works, and the ravages of an adventurous life were beginning to take their toll on his physical body—Hunter S. Thompson would often invite younger writers to his house. He reportedly did this because their enthusiasm for a craft and a business which had not yet broken their hearts, and their gratitude toward him, often re-energized him and his muse, no matter how temporary.

Last Saturday, I was lucky enough to have authors John Goodrich and Adam Cesare join us here in my home recording studio so that Dave and I could interview them for upcoming episodes of my podcast, *The Horror Show with Brian Keene*. But the day turned into a mini-convention, with authors Scott Cole,

Stephen Kozeniewski, and Mary SanGiovanni, filmmaker Mike Lombardo, super-fans Kevin and Kristen Foster, and Dave's girlfriend "Phoebe" joining us, as well.

I won't lie. After a few years of soul-searching, second-guessing, burning out, burning down, and wondering if anything I did actually fucking mattered while everyone around me seemed to be dying, it was nice to have a home full of younger or newer writers and artists who seemed genuinely appreciative and grateful and full of good spirits and hope.

I found their presence—along with that of a few old friends—provided a little warmth against the snow that continues to fall outside. It's nice to know that maybe some of it mattered, and maybe a few folks will remember you when you're gone.

After recording, we all took a field trip to The York Emporium. Some of J. F. Gonzalez's ashes are kept there. The kids all wanted to visit him, and pay homage. While browsing through the shelves, I found three signed copies of John Skipp and Craig Spector's *The Light at the End*—one of the absolute classics of the splatterpunk sub-genre. I made sure Adam, Scott, and Mike each went home with one, and I felt a real sense of history as I handed those books to them—three generations of horror writers, one generation after the other, helping each other and all hoping for the same thing.

On Sunday, Mike Lombardo and I finished a year-long task of moving all of J. F. Gonzalez's papers, books, and private effects. While going through boxes, J. F.'s wife, Cathy, found a bunch of hand-written letters from Robert Bloch to J. F., Mike Baker, and Mark Williams. None of those four authors are with us now, and my time is probably limited, but it pleased me that Mike understood the importance of those letters, and why they mattered, and why the people in them mattered, and the generational sense of history that was imbued in them.

Outside, it's snowing again. I'm sitting here writing, and

thinking—supposedly alone, and yet surrounded by others. Surrounded by a history that I've somehow become a part of.

Yes, sir, I will answer when asked. I have my scars, and they've made a mark.

But I've made a mark of my own, as well.

UNSAFE SPACES

This was a book about dying.

I didn't realize any of that at the time these essays and Blog entries and appreciations and remembrances were written, of course (which was back in the years 2014 through early 2016). Oh no. I didn't realize it until I began compiling all of that material together and going through the long, laborious process of editing it. A process made more painful by the fact that it seems like every other entry was a variation on the theme of 'My Friends Keep Dying On Me" by Brian Keene.

The book opens fine, but very quickly, someone is dead. I didn't talk about it much at the beginning, so I'll talk about it here at the end, instead. (And tif this isn't enough for you, I've since written a novel-length book about it called *End of the Road*).

Anyway, on a warm August day in 2014, Mary SanGiovanni and I were deep in the middle of the New Jersey Pine Barrens, exploring the region so that she could get some background research for a novel she was working on. When we got to an area with cell phone service, my phone rang. It was my second ex-wife, and she was distraught. I immediately thought something had happened to our son, but instead, was stunned to learn that a mutual friend of ours, Jason, had died of a sudden brain aneurysm.

Jason and I had been best friends for years. We were friends long before I ever became a writer—but the last few of those years were turbulent. You see, Jason and I made up two corners of a lover's square. My second ex-wife and Mary made up the other two corners. Two guys, two women, and one big fucking mess. He and I stopped speaking altogether for a while, and when we did finally try to make peace with each other, it was forced and slow-going.

We were still working our way through all of that when he died, and now I get to live with everything that was left unsaid, and unsettled. But my grief is a small thing. He left behind two young sons, a mother, two sisters, a bunch of mutual friends, and a woman who loved him—a woman who is important to me, as well. I feel for all of them, and it puts my trivial pain in perspective. Still, it's not the sort of thing you want to see jump out at you from the space between the pages of the book you're working on.

And then it happens again, with Graham Joyce. Now, I can't profess that I was a close, personal friend of Graham's, because I wasn't. We were professional acquaintances, but we got on well enough, and I enjoyed the few times I hung out with him over the years. He was, however, a very close friend of several people I consider very close friends, particularly Sarah Pinborough, Tim Lebbon, and Mark Morris. Their loss is my loss, as it is for the rest of our mutual support network. And it's a loss for the genre, as well.

Halfway through the book, Jesus Gonzalez dies. That happened quick, in retrospect. From his initial diagnosis ("Hey, Brian You'll have to work on *Libra Nigrum Scientia Secreta* today, because I have to go to the doctor for a check-up") to the moment his heart monitor went flat-line, it was just a little over one month. I watched that motherfucking cancer whittle him down to nothing. That was the scariest aspect, to be honest—the speed at which he deteriorated.

And yet, the weeks preceding his death are here, in this book. His fate is lurking in the spaces between the words. I can see it. I suspect if you go back and re-read it, you'll see it, too.

Jesus was a card-carrying liberal. Among the things he despised with a passion was FOX News. The last practical joke I ever played on him (and we played jokes on each other all the fucking time) was two days before he died. We'd gone to the hospital to visit him. He couldn't talk, because he had a breathing tube down his throat, but he could write (his wife had gotten him a dry erase board to use to communicate with everyone), and he was alert, and able to see the television. When it was time for me to leave, I squeezed his hand and told him that I loved him. He squeezed my hand back and his eyes said the same. Those eyes were droopy and heavy-lidded I knew he'd probably be asleep before I even made it to the ground floor. As it turned out, it didn't even take that long He was asleep before I'd reached the door to his hospital room. Upon seeing this, I turned around, crept back inside, and turned his television to the FOX News Channel, so it would be on when he woke up. I remember grinning and giggling at this grand practical joke.

I also remember that the FOX News anchor was talking about the creation of so-called "safe spaces" on college campuses.

Safe spaces...

Just as I was starting to come to grips with Jesus's death (as much as you can over come to grips with losing somebody you were that close to), Tom Piccirilli died.

Now, unlike Jesus, Pic was sick for a long time. He'd had the brain cancer once before, and it had supposedly been terminal at that point, and all of us had gone to see him and tell him goodbye (that story is recounted in *Trigger Warnings*). We were overjoyed when he beat the cancer, and distraught when it returned. His death hit me hard, but it affected me in a much different way than Jesus's did, and I'm still not sure I understand why. I loved Pic. He really was like a big brother to me. And yet, I guess somewhere deep down inside, I suspected it would happen. I guess after Jason and Jesus and everyone else, I assumed it would come. I cried when he was gone, but I didn't drink myself into oblivion and stop writing the way I'd done when Jesus passed.

Jason, Jesus, Pic—each of their deaths impacted me in a different way, and I dealt with and processed each of them in different ways.

But the one thing I did in all three cases was write about them. And even when I wasn't consciously writing about them, even when I was supposedly writing about some dingbat on the internet or some unscrupulous publisher or something my son and I had done or a trip to a real-life ghost town—even then, I was writing about Jason and Jesus and Pic. Even then, they were lurking in the spaces between the words.

The world is an unsafe space. Space is an unsafe space. Our hearts and minds are an unsafe space. But the blanks spaces between the words you're reading?

That's the most unsafe space of all.

Thanks for buying this book, and all of my other books. I appreciate your continued support. It means as much to me now as it did twenty years ago, when we started out together. I hope you'll stick around for the rest of the ride. The coaster is definitely slowing down, and we're a long way from start and there's no going back, but I suspect there may still be a few hills and loops and thrills left to experience together.

And if not, then just know that it has been my honor to have you as a companion on this ride, dear reader.

Now, hang on tight. It looks like we're about to head into a tunnel again. What do you think? Do you think there will be a light at the end of it?

Let's find out.

ABOUT THE AUTHOR

BRIAN KEENE writes novels, comic books, stories, journalism, and other words for money. He is the author of over fifty books, mostly in the horror, crime, and dark fantasy genres.

His 2003 novel, *The Rising*, is credited (along with Robert Kirkman's *The Walking Dead* comic and Danny Boyle's *28 Days Later* film) with inspiring pop culture's recurrent interest in zombies. Keene's books have been translated into German, Spanish, Russian, Polish, Italian, French, Taiwanese, and many other languages. He oversees Maelstrom, a small press publishing imprint specializing in collectible limited editions, via Thunderstorm Books.

He has written for such Marvel and DC properties as *Thor, Doom Patrol, Justice League, Harley Quinn, Devil-Slayer, Superman, and Masters of the Universe*, as well as his own critically acclaimed creator-owned comic series *The Last Zombie*. Keene has also written for media properties such as *Doctor Who*, *The X-Files*, *Hellboy*, and *Aliens*.

Keene also hosts the popular podcasts *The Horror Show with Brian Keene* and *Defenders Dialogue*, both of which air weekly on iTunes, Spotify, Stitcher, YouTube, and elsewhere.

Several of Keene's novels and stories have been adapted for film, including *Ghoul*, *The Naughty List*, *The Ties That Bind*, and *Fast Zombies Suck*. Several more are in-development. Keene also served as Executive Producer for the feature length film *I'm Dreaming of a White Doomsday*.

Keene's work has been praised by *The New York Times*, *The History Channel*, *The Howard Stern Show*, *CNN*, *The Huffington Post*, *Bleeding Cool*, *Publisher's Weekly*, *Fangoria*, *Bloody Disgusting*, and *Rue Morgue*.

His numerous awards and honors include the 2014 World Horror Grandmaster Award, 2001 Bram Stoker Award for Nonfiction, 2003 Bram Stoker Award for First Novel, the 2016 Imadjinn Award for Best Fantasy Novel, the 2015 Imaginarium Film Festival Awards for Best Screenplay, Best Short Film Genre, and Best Short Film Overall, the 2004 Shocker Award for Book of the Year, and Honors from United States Army International Security Assistance Force in Afghanistan and Whiteman A.F.B. (home of the B-2 Stealth Bomber) 509th Logistics Fuels Flight. A prolific public speaker, Keene has delivered talks at conventions, college campuses, theaters, and inside Central Intelligence Agency headquarters in Langley, VA.

Keene serves on the Board of Directors for the Scares That Care 501c charity organization.

The father of two sons, Keene lives in rural Pennsylvania with author Mary SanGiovanni.

Printed in Poland
by Amazon Fulfillment
Poland Sp. z o.o., Wrocław